KT-472-272

# Redress

# Redress

Adèle Hartley

burninghouse

First published 2007

A Burning House book

www.burninghousebooks.com

Burning House is an imprint of
Beautiful Books Limited
117 Sugden Road
London SW11 5ED

ISBN 9781905636099

9 8 7 6 5 4 3 2 1

Cover by Head Design
Printed in the UK by Mackays of Chatham.

*For Olive*

*with love*

*(and automatic washing machines)*

*Acknowledgements*

With love and thanks to Iain, Carrie Bishop,
Nancy Currie, Kier-la Janisse, Lara Matthews
and Christine Slatter.

Thanks to my family and more good friends than I can
list for their interest and invaluable support and
to Simon and Tamsin at Beautiful Books
for not just creating glorious opportunities,
but realising them with such commitment
and enthusiasm.

I am grateful to both David Powell and Mary Ann
Gamboa who gave their expertise and time, and
especially to Beverley Koven for her local
knowledge, kindness and generosity.

Finally, I owe so much, with love, to the unique
Sara Sharpe, a fine writer and wonderful friend
without whom none of this would
ever have happened.

# PART ONE

# Chapter Zero

Skirving hated the heat.

It made him sleepy and irritable and Skirving couldn't sleep when he was irritable. More than the heat, he hated the sweat. It was pooling in the small of his back and under his arms. There were clingy damp patches all over his shirt and the crease of his long shorts at the back of his knees was drenched; the waistband a wet, itchy belt around him. He felt like tiny ants were crawling around inside his clothes. All day his eyes had been stinging as the salt ran from his forehead. The one thing he hated more than the sweat was air-conditioning because it made him sneeze, but after the day's exertions that was a price he was willing to pay.

It amused Skirving how distorted the kitchen looked from the floor. Both still as night, he and Nell lay on the delicious cool of the kitchen tiles. She was out for the count but with the windows shut and pale yellow blinds drawn against the sun, Skirving enjoyed letting the air-conditioner slather the exposed skin of his arms in goose-bumps. The machine's hypnotic hum lulled him to the hazy verge of a doze, the only thought troubling him was that he might be hungry again.

The heat did odd things to Skirving's appetite. For breakfast he'd carved a huge slice of watermelon from the half in the fridge. Super-chilled, it sent little cold spikes of pain ricocheting around his teeth. Each icy sliver seemed to find a rotten crevice, making lurking raw nerves twitch at the freezing intrusion. To warm his mouth he'd wolfed down an entire pack of sugared cherry cakes which he now swore he could feel individually fidgeting in his stomach, trying to get comfy. What he really fancied was a hotdog with lots of slimy, oily, tangy onions and an enormous glass of iced tea.

He whispered to an oblivious Nell, 'I'm having cravings,' then giggled his high little giggle, and rested his head onto the crook of his elbow. The cherry cakes grumbled, plumped their pillows and settled down again.

Skirving couldn't eat sensibly at Nell's place because her roommate Trish didn't shop sensibly. Trish frequently extolled the virtues of being able to shop drunk at 4 a.m., thereby having the store to herself. More importantly, it meant there was no-one to tut disapprovingly when she took a notion to fondle all the fruit, or fall over the aisle displays or, once, curl up and go to sleep amongst the soft rolls of toilet paper. Trish was the reason the refrigerator was stocked with munchie-food but little else, unless you counted the number of times Skirving had opened the door only to see a shoe or purse or car keys lurking amongst the cookies and hummus and giant tubs of novelty mallows. He'd found the cat's food bowl in there so often that the truculent beast had long since gone to live with the upstairs neighbour.

However, with Trish gone on assignment, he and Nell had the apartment to themselves for two days so, the previous evening, they'd meandered round the store hand-in-hand, choosing all the things they loved, and all manner of indulgences that an uninterrupted weekend justified.

Reaching out one hand, Skirving gently brushed a stray hair from Nell's face. Even here, out cold on the kitchen floor, she took his breath away. When he'd first seen her, like a stumbling adolescent, he hadn't known where to look. Sure like most guys he had a 'type' but you hardly expected your ideal woman to just walk up to you with a drop-dead smile and start talking, but that's exactly what she'd done.

Of course later, over a coffee, they'd both laughed at her mistake. She had been so sure she'd known him, so sure they'd met before, but here she was, talking to a complete stranger.

While they'd chatted that day, Skirving had wanted nothing more than to reach out and stroke her skin. It was smooth and pale and every time she laughed, tiny dimples appeared around her mouth. Her thick straw-blonde hair shook as she spoke, the wide curls dancing on her shoulders.

He just couldn't believe his luck. She was a gift. In Nell he found exactly what he'd been looking for and knew in his heart that everything was going to be just fine from then on. He had sipped at his coffee, waited for his moment, then asked if he could take her to dinner the next night. Of course she said yes.

From then on, life with her had been easy. So many things had fallen naturally into place that he was horrified how previous relationships seemed to have involved so much work, so much compromise. Nell was the right answer to questions he had asked for so very long.

Now he watched her eyes begin to move beneath the lids, heard her breathing change, listened to the tiny sounds that escaped her as she slid through cloud towards waking. As her eyes flickered open, he gloried in the flecks of gold that seemed to make her blue irises shine.

Skirving made sure that the first thing Nell ever saw on waking was his smile, and he intended today to be no different. He watched her face, wishing he could recall just how beautiful it had been. His memory failed him, derailed by the torn and splintered ruins of her nose and mouth.

He leaned into her, taking great care to avoid the pooling slicks of warm blood that settled the plastic sheeting into the grooves between the tiles. He watched as her eyes focused in recognition and widened in remembrance.

His breathing was almost as shallow and ragged as hers when he spoke.

'Honey, listen to me very carefully because you don't have long. There's something I need you to hear.'

He paused, wishing her panicked, stuttered and wet breathing would subside. Every one of Nell's frantic attempts to draw a clean breath wrenched her broken body with increasingly violent spasms, haemorrhaging beyond repair with every shudder.

She tried reaching for him but he moved away each time, staring at her outstretched hand. He couldn't bear to touch her clammy flesh. Taking a deep breath to compose himself, he held his finger up to shush her. Nell's body sank back, little bubbles of drool and blood foaming at the corners of her mouth.

'You are…you were…I wanted everything for

us, do you understand that? You and I were meant for each other and we could have been together forever, you know?' Skirving shook his head, raising his eyebrows, admonishing her. 'If only you'd let me, there's nothing I wouldn't have done to make it all perfect. We could have stayed here, stayed together, but you screwed that up. If only you'd thought to…'

She blinked and in the search for the right word, he lost his momentum. He sat back, for a few moments feeling the air-conditioning chill his sweat-slicked skin, shivering a little in the cold. It helped calm him enough to concentrate on regulating his breathing. He needed to collect his thoughts; her time was running short. More than anything he wanted to remember their final moments together with clarity.

Skirving looked down as he heard her breathing falter. As her eyelids flickered, he scrambled to his knees, the plastic sheeting beneath him crackling with the sudden movement. He stuck his face in hers one last time and hissed,

'Be grateful, bitch. I should have burned you.'

He rocked back against the kitchen wall, exhilarated but exhausted, watching as the light faded from her eyes. Without waiting to see her die, Skirving pushed himself to his feet, stretched and cracked his knuckles. From where he stood, he took a careful look around the room one last time. Satisfied that he'd left nothing of consequence, he peeled off his caked latex gloves, turned them inside-out and carefully slipped them into a lined open side pocket of his small rucksack, tucking the extra plastic around them before closing the zip and slinging the bag over his shoulder.

He walked on unsoiled plastic sheeting to the rear porch door where he stepped into a pair of Wal-Mart special offer sneakers bought sometime the summer before. Once outside, he folded the clean sheeting behind him, packed it away and without looking back, walked calmly down the old wooden steps and across the carefully tended back garden. At the fence, he slipped through a gap into the lane where the overhead power-lines buzzed like a frenzied cricket chorus. A glimpse in both directions confirmed there was no-one in sight and, smiling to himself, he made his way to the nearest bus stop.

In less than an hour he boarded his train and was comfortably asleep when they crossed the state line. Woken a little after midnight at the border, neither he nor his papers merited more than a glance by the bored patrol. By then he had decided that he liked the sound of Skirving and would keep the name for use another time.

Less than twenty-four hours after Skirving crossed into

North America, Trish Delaney returned exhausted from an assignment up the coast in Boston.

An eleven-hour delay for an hour's flight was bad enough, but being joined in the departure lounge by two hundred Holy Joes had done little for her mood. When first approached, she'd shuddered at the woman's loose green smock and corn-row hair, but it was the four-inch square yellow badge pinned squint above her baggy breast that really did it. In large, supposedly friendly lettering it read, 'Teacher of the Word of God'. Trish had slugged a mouthful of beer from the bottle and stared with extraordinary intensity at a sticky patch on the bar right in front of her, thinking 'fuck-off' vibes just as hard as she could. She could feel the woman's stale breath on her cheek. So this was how it had to be. Those vibes that had consistently failed with greasy men in greasier bars and in stores with chirpy, over-enthusiastic assistants were now abandoning her to religious fanatics, too. She wished she was better at crap like this.

The nice lady laid a hand on Trish's shoulder, ignored the flinch and made puppy eyes at her before handing out a sheet of song lyrics and moving on to the next sucker, who looked like he was contemplating faking a fit to get away.

The singing started twenty minutes later and lasted the remaining nine hours of the delay, the entire eighty five minutes of the flight and the half-hour Trish had to wait at the dormant luggage carousel in La Guardia. As it finally started moving, the nice lady had approached again and asked if she could pray for Trish. The answer would not have made Jesus happy, but the woman prayed anyway, right up until Trish's bag appeared, making her wonder if the woman had prayed for it to come last.

By the time she was in the back of a cab leaving the airport, she was verging on incoherent and had tried calling Nell but got nothing more than the answer machine. It didn't matter. By that point Trish knew she would tell an eggplant her woes if it would just look like it was listening to her. She ranted on.

'Nothing but steamed veg. Salad. More salad than you can shake a model at. Seriously man, those chicks are so thin they must keep their damn spleens in their handbags because there's sure as hell no room in their tiny, flat bodies. I've seen wider shoelaces. Every meal is grilled bloody chicken and fish. It'd be more fun frying the curtains and eating them. Tonight, I swear I am having a family-sized bucket of fried chicken. All to myself. Not only that, I'm gonna ask them to cover it in batter again and fry the hell out of it a second time. And it had better come with a mountain of fries. And a coke. A whole, full-fat, ohmigawd full-of-calories coke. And then a goddamn bucket of ice-cream. And then I am going to lie around in my PJs trying to see the TV over the gross, distended mound of my belly. And if I can still breathe unaided, I'm gonna follow it up with those deep-fried Jalapeno peppers stuffed with cheese and dipped in that totally evil scarlet toxic dip that probably glows in the dark.'

Skirving had listened to the machine from the kitchen, wishing she would be quiet.

At the third insistent beep of her dying battery, Trish hung up and went back to muttering under her breath the mantra that had kept her sane all the way home after four days managing the egos of whining models.

'Cold beer. Pie. Lots of chocolate. Cold beer. Pie. Lots of chocolate. Cold beer...'

She didn't stop chanting until she opened their front door and stopped on the threshold, all thoughts of food forgotten as she gagged at the smell that pushed its way past her and into the late Summer heat.

'Jesus, girl,' she muttered, 'what died?'

Within the hour, Trish was being comforted by a female cop in her living room, while two Homicide detectives and a forensics team swarmed over the small kitchen.

Doug McLeod had picked up his mail and gone straight back to bed that morning. He lay listening to whiny Country music from his neighbour's radio while he waded through the junk hoping for some genuine contact from the outside world. Apart from three scams offering him millions if only he'd call this premium-rate number, there was just what looked like a letter from his sister Susie and a bank statement. All things being relative, Doug saved the best for last and opened his sister's letter first.

A cursory glance yielded everything he expected. With their mother long dead, Susie had taken over the mantle of Chief Nag of the McLeod dynasty to ensure that Doug never had to go six months without a bullet-point reminder of his failings as a son, brother and uncle. He scanned the family news, balked at the suggestion he spend Thanksgiving with them, muttered 'love you too, sis', before scrunching the letter into a tight ball and throwing it across the room. It joined the pile of crumpled paper forming a halo around his trash.

The shape of his financial affairs didn't make him any happier. Grimacing at his statement, he turned over and tried to get back to sleep, grumbling a wish for the financial bonus that some decent murder-enquiry overtime would bring.

Standing by Nell Donaldson's kitchen window

two hours later, Doug wished he'd been a little more circumspect with his desires. He glanced upwards and muttered, mostly to himself, 'I meant one of those nice clean murders, you bastards. You know, one gunshot, no witnesses, a month of futile searching and then a badly bundled parcel of papers on its way to the Cold Case Unit and I can afford to go to Hawaii for a week. That kind of murder. Not this shit. This sucks the big one.' Doug was certain he could hear karma sniggering.

He scratched the side of his nose, let out a very long sigh and drained the foul dregs of his long-cold coffee.

Four years before Doug added Nell Donaldson to his nightmares, Illinois security guard Steve Bassing had waited for paramedics, helpless, as a blonde and blue-eyed girl called Emily had choked to death on the floor at his feet. The gurgling noises made him nauseous and, with no proper training, all he could do was make futile attempts to calm her each time her frantic hands grabbed at him, her eyes wide and panicked.

A week earlier, her new boyfriend had leant down on her neck way too hard in the throes of orgasm. It had been sore for a few days, but her doctor was unconcerned, citing some other unlikely-sounding accidents of passion he'd seen over the years, then told her the bruising and redness would fade. His parting suggestion was that maybe she should go on top next time.

Less than a week later her fractured and fatally weakened hyoid bone finally snapped in a shoe store on a quiet Thursday morning, choking her to death in under a minute.

The morning of her burial, Skirving stood at the back of the small crowd of mourners, watching Emily's parents say goodbye to their only daughter. He wanted to tell them how much potential she had, how good his intentions had been, how much he intended to love her. But he couldn't, because then he would have had to tell them how badly she had disappointed him, how obstructive she was and how thwarted all his attempts had been. The slut was simply too stupid to know what was good for her.

The man next to him turned and stared, briefly, and Skirving froze. Had he said that aloud? He waited a moment but no-one else turned his way. Before the service concluded he backed off, leaving the cemetery by a side gate and heading for the bus station, there to collect his stored luggage and head South-East.

Eighteen months later, a Virginian cop called Matt Tyler was called to a condo in Richmond. Both her immediate neighbours knew that the single woman who lived there had a new man in her life, but beyond that all he got was that the guy was average height, average build and had brown hair. Matt knew the investigation was over pretty much before it began unless something major turned up. The other tenants confirmed what he knew before he asked – the woman had seemed shy, kept herself to herself, worked from home. She had always been a quiet and responsible tenant, civil to her neighbours whenever they met on the stairs. What the cops found was a woman who had chewed her tongue into a ragged pulp before drowning in her own blood. It was clear from her secondary injuries that she hadn't died quickly.

After the autopsy revealed that she had been dealt a single lethal dose of an Atropine compound, a hunch made Tyler have the contents of her fridge tested. They found traces of Belladonna extract in everything. With few prints, no clear description of male visitors, no known enemies and a poison that grew naturally in abundance, Matt was left with a slab-cold trail. The curiosity of the torture was his only hope for an MO match down the line after filing the lonely, vicious, unsolved end of Rachel's life with the Cold Case Unit.

Steve Bassing and Matt Tyler were the only two men in the world who might have been able to help Doug right now, but the three men would never meet. Each one carried his own demons, haunted by cruelty and pain, each one coping in ways that made it possible for them to carry on with their scars carefully hidden.

Doug's first cursory glance at the victim had been more than enough so early in the day and made him wish he hadn't eaten. He knew it was gonna take two fat fingers of Johnny Red to make the day better when he got home.

The problem with a weird death like Nell Donaldson's was that his boss would be breathing down his neck, panicking about press interest and demanding a result he could announce with pride and sod-all credit to the investigating officer. A regular homicide investigation wouldn't be enough to keep that man happy and Doug knew he was about forty eight hours away from having to bring in some quack with topical theories about ritual mutilation and god only knows what else. What he resented most of all was interference from those idiots who always had their eye on the prize of a book and movie deal, and already knew what they'd wear when the call came from Oprah. Doug growled. He wanted this done in-house and quickly.

'Fucking parasites,' he growled again and swept

the sweat from the sides of his nose, wiping damp hands on his damp shirt.

Doug's partner Daniel was back through in the living room trying with little success to get some sense out the roommate and Doug could hear Dan's steady, calm voice cut through the sobbing. He would have to join him soon but for the moment he stayed in the kitchen watching Forensics do their thing. He'd already broken the golden rule and looked at the victim's face and knew he didn't have a chance in hell of getting to sleep that night.

Make that three fingers, Johnny boy, he thought.

'Doug?'

'Jesus, man, how can you eat at a time like this? You're a freak.'

The coroner licked his lips and grinned, revealing teeth speckled with poppy seeds. Doug's brain obliged him with a clear sensory reminder of the eggs and bacon he'd wolfed down before the call came. He swallowed hard, but all he could feel was the memory of opaque, slippery albumen skimming over his tongue.

He cleared his throat and pictured himself out on the lake come the weekend with nothing to see but sky and mountains and with a bit of luck, no fish to disturb the peace of mind that fishing gave him.

With effort, he derailed the queasy uprising.

'Want a bite?' asked Andy, sniggering as he proffered the last chunk of his pastrami bagel.

'Bastard,' snarled Doug, swallowing hard and trying to think of fluffy pink clouds, but now all he could picture were bloated lilac corpses and he tasted bile burning the back of his throat. He grimaced at the coroner.

'Come on then, Barbie, do your worst.'

'Is that ever gonna stop amusing the hell outta you?'

'You know, I don't think it is.'

'Suit yourself,' said Andy, popping the last of his breakfast into his mouth and chewing loudly as he looked over the body. He made big lip-smacking noises at Doug before getting on with it.

'Open and shut case, my friend,' he said, walking around the corpse and looking back at the now pale cop. 'Guy you're looking for is tall, tired-looking, died in sixteen-something or other, goes by the name of Matthew Hopkins.'

Doug leant back, resting his elbows on the low window sill. He raised greying eyebrows at the coroner and waited.

'Witchfinder General to you and me, Doug,' Andy went on, ignoring the scathing glare and snort of derision that came his way.

'I'm serious,' he said, licking his fingers and pulling on latex gloves, dropping down to his knees. 'She's been tortured for being a witch. Burning her's the only thing he hasn't done.'

Doug wasn't often lost for words. He stared at the immaculately combed back of Andy's head while the coroner acknowledged a colleague and took hold of a bagged item, keeping it out of sight for the moment. Doug could wait. He knew that whatever it was, once he'd seen it, no matter how hard he tried, he'd never shift the image from the ever-expanding gallery of the grotesque that filled his mind.

'A witch?' He wanted to laugh, but there was nothing funny in the room.

Andy, now stood beside him, touched Doug lightly on the elbow, angling him around the corpse, being careful not to get in the way of the photographer.

'See – the markings on her throat there…and there?' he pointed, and Doug looked past the abrasions and contusions he'd seen on his first quick inspection, now seeing for the first time some finer red lines and patches over the victim's neck.

'Willing to bet you a crisp twenty the autopsy finds a couple obstructions in her oesophagus. He used something hot – whatever the twenty-first century equivalent of burning coals is – maybe heated glass or boiling oil. Whatever he fed her, it did a pretty good job of scalding her lips, tongue and throat, most likely so she couldn't speak any more. That black stuff around her mouth isn't all blood.'

Doug nodded, breathing slowly and deliberately through his mouth, trying hard not to imagine the woman's final hours on earth. He fumbled for his cigarettes, only remembering too late that he'd quit. He muttered furious curses to a God he didn't believe in and stuck his hands deep into his empty pockets.

Without being asked, Andy passed him a stick of gum, then walked Doug the long way around the body. As soon as he got a good look, Doug knew what was in the bag. On reflex he ran his hand through his hair. Andy knelt, looked up at Doug to ensure he had his full attention, then pointed to the back of the woman's head as one of his assistants lifted her hair aside.

'He knotted her. I've seen variations of this over the years, but usually with a vice. He's strong, Doug. Or very angry. Or both. Look...' and he stood to show Doug the bag.

Doug saw the piece of pink scalp clearly, saw the patches of black where clotting blood made Rorschach patterns flicker before his tired eyes. The mass of blonde hair, matted with blood and opaque fluid, was wound tightly around what looked like a chopstick. Stuck to the inside of the bag were shards of bone and small wet bits of pink matter.

'Four fingers, Johnny,' muttered Doug to himself.

'Apparently,' said the coroner with a little more enthusiasm than Doug thought appropriate, 'when this was common practice there would come a point when one person wasn't strong enough to turn this any harder,' he said, touching the stick through the plastic, 'so they'd put the victim's head in a vice and get some muscle to actually do the dirty work. The whole point is to twist it enough to pull a piece of scalp away.'

Andy paused, lowering the bag to his side. 'What gets me is that he didn't feed any of it to her. Or take it with him. You know, the whole trophy thing. In fact,' he went on, 'she doesn't seem to be missing anything at all.'

'And the face?' Doug asked.

'Scoring. It used to be called *scoring above the breath*. Again, there's lots of ways of bleeding someone to death slowly – you'd be surprised how many...we're seriously badly designed. I mean, you can choose to do it the quick way but it's just lazy. I saw a guy once, slit from groin to gullet and...'

Andy stopped, melting under Doug's glare.

'So...' Andy shuffled his feet like a chastised kid

before continuing, 'like I was saying, the stylised mutilation seems pretty important here. She wasn't a bad-looking woman. Such a waste. Anyway, he's cut her four times with something simple like a cut-throat, then turned her over to bleed out.'

Doug resigned himself to going to the liquor store on the way home.

'And before you ask,' said Andy peeling off his gloves and passing them to his assistant, before wiping a stray smear of mustard from his chin, 'I've only ever seen this shit in books. Well done, Douglas, you finally got a bona fide weirdo on your turf.'

# Chapter One

'You've got a garden.'

'It's *not* a garden, Mick, it's a window box.'

'S'got plants in it.'

Kath dropped the property pages into her husband's lap, lightly slapped him across the back of his head and ducked out the way of his feeble retaliation.

'At least take a look,' she said, turning in the doorway, 'a twenty-minute ride into the city is such a small price to pay, honey, really.'

Which is how, six months later, Cassie's parents found themselves moving to Scarborough, a new neighbourhood on the GO Line with good schools, a large park and lots of other kids Cassie's age. They had visions of her roller-skating the safe streets with her new friends and playing T–Ball on the lawn.

With street after unpaved street of ranch-style houses and a Pontiac in practically every drive, they'd been there a week when one of the moms waiting with Kath outside the school shared the news that downtown Toronto liked to indulge in bouts of urbanite sneering, referring to the area as Scarberia. Kath, who didn't go to sleep lulled by the sound of midnight sirens any more, just didn't care.

They'd been there ten months when the 'Sale' sign outside the house next door was taken away. Not long after that, the Holliers moved in and a couple days later, Kath went to introduce herself to Mary. What started as pleasantries over the hedges soon moved to Kath's back garden with coffee, cookies and confessions.

'I'd have been quite happy to stay in the city, but Jen scuppered that idea.'

'She wasn't planned?'

'God, no. I guess "late surprise" is the most tactful way to put it. Serves us right for getting stoned and making out like careless teenagers, I guess. Although it did take about a week for all the panic, blame, shock, histrionics, sulking and crying to subside,' Mary laughed. 'Once we started breathing again we figured if we didn't eat much, wear anything new or go anyplace for around a decade, we could totally afford to have a baby.'

Mary paused only to look up at Jen's bedroom window. 'I guess the gods smiled on us, though, because she slept all night, smiled all day and barely cried. She was exactly the kind of curious, gentle, calm child that no-one seriously expects to have.'

Kath groaned aloud. 'So that's where Cassie's calm went. I think we got all your crazy.'

'You can keep it! Anyway, last Fall we got down to some serious house-hunting and here we all are and according to you, apparently exiled to Scarberia! All I need now is for Jen to find lots of other kids to play with so she stops asking about getting a brother or sister for Christmas or for her birthday or because it's Tuesday.'

'Ohmigawd,' laughed Kath. 'You too? Though Cassie wants subjects, not siblings. I was so totally convinced that with a move out here we had a good chance of getting her to meet other kids.'

'It didn't work?'

Kath raised her eyebrows. 'Lemme tell you something…on one now legendary occasion that took half a day's pleading and the kind of threats that would reduce a seasoned Child Services officer to a gibbering wreck, I got Cassie out her beloved tree and into the park. Once there, my charming daughter climbed a completely different tree and refused to come down till all the other kids had gone home.'

'Ah. Not good. Well, Jen spends so much time with her nose in a book I'm not even sure she knows we've moved house.'

'Cassie thinks books are for helping her reach the cookie jar. Or propping doors open.'

'Don't get me wrong,' said Mary quickly, 'it's not that we're ungrateful, it's just that she seems oblivious to the rest of the world.'

'Fine,' grinned Kath. 'Ten bucks says they're inseparable by the weekend.'

# Chapter Two

One Spring, with my birthday coming up, my parents decided they wanted a dog. They kept telling me how good it would be to have a dog as if somehow they could make it my idea.

Back then we lived on the third floor so my parents spent a couple of weeks sweet-talking the grumpy Super into saying yes. My mother even baked for the cantankerous old fool, when all he really cared about was that the dog wouldn't bark or crap in the elevator. Eventually, where their promises weren't enough, their money was.

Once he said yes, my parents dragged me along to an animal shelter and picked one out. They kept asking me what I thought I would like, what kind, what sex, but I didn't care. They wanted the dog and I was their excuse.

I lost count of how many cages we walked past. Some of the dogs barked and jumped at the wire when they saw us, some lay on the floor, only raising dead eyes to watch us go by, seeming to know that rejection was inevitable. On the way home, my parents seemed pretty pleased with themselves for having saved this one dog from being put to sleep, but all I could think was how that made all the other dogs feel knowing they were probably going to die for not being cute enough. I wondered if they knew just how screwed they were. I mean, there are homes for kids that nobody wants, but they don't get killed after seven days, they just get to grow up to be adults that nobody wants.

When I eventually pointed at the sleepy-eyed Dalmation, the woman from the shelter started telling me what a good choice I'd made and what a sweet friend he'd be. I tried to look like I was pleased but really I just wanted to go home.

My mom and dad filled out a mountain of paperwork and came away with a lot of fliers about dog care and vet costs and kennels for when we went on vacation. I could see my dad had already changed his mind and thought the dog was gonna be too much work but he mostly kept it to himself.

On the way back, my parents asked me to name him, like that would make him more my pet, but I didn't really care. I called him Dog. Mom and Dad both pretended they thought that was cute.

They went to pick up the mutt a couple of days later.

One super-hot afternoon that summer we were all indoors to have lunch. As ever, the crappy air-conditioning was out so we had all the windows open but that seemed to let more heat in, not out.

As I was clearing up, my parents got into some stupid fight about the air-conditioning and my dad stormed off to the bar downstairs. My mom sulked so hard she seemed to forget all about me so I spent the afternoon on the sofa just watching cartoons. Dog was all splayed out on the floor, panting like crazy. Me and him, we didn't move the whole damn day.

I knew it was rush hour because the traffic got so loud I couldn't hear the TV even with the sound turned way up. I went to go close the window but just as my butt left the sofa, a tiny bird flew down and settled on our ledge. Dog's paws skittered on the wood floor as he scrambled frantically to gain some purchase and I thought he was going to start barking like he did at the park – he was always weird about birds, trying to scare them off and catch them at the same time. But this time he didn't bark. As I turned to watch him, he just stared at the little bird for about a minute, looked straight at me, then ran right across the room and jumped at it, his mouth wide open.

At the last minute the bird flew away but by then it was too late for Dog to stop and he sailed right out the window.

When I looked over the edge it was like he had burst.

I fucking hated that dumb-ass dog.

# Chapter Three

'If you can lick your own elbow, you're not a boy.'

Cassie, having been told to go find other kids to play with, had got as far as the kerb. She'd been sulking there most of an hour just rubbing the muddy patches on her dungarees until she'd obliterated all the clean spots. Hearing voices nearby she peeked through her fringe and was dismayed to see pink flip-flopped feet scuff across the street towards her. She had let out a deep sigh as she looked up.

Heather Mackie stood defiant before her. She wore jeans with a ribbon belt and a sequinned butter-fly patch on each pocket. Her t-shirt, like her shoes, was pink and clean, a sure sign she'd be no fun to play with. Her waist-length blonde, shiny, perfectly straight hair swung in matching pigtails tied with pink ribbon, and the dozen pink bangles on her wrists made her rattle when she skipped. Hands on hips, she waited for a response.

Looking past her across the street, Cassie saw three identical blondes huddled under the Mackie's tree watching to see if the new kid would rise to their latest dumb challenge.

Cassie's mood plummeted to a record low. She fixed Heather with her hardest stare. 'What?'

'Look,' said the creature with pigtails, grabbing her own arm, twisting it around and pulling it towards her straining tongue. Cassie could only watch as the scarlet tongue-tip briefly connected with its target, leaving a sticky sugar-smear across otherwise unblemished skin.

'See?' panted Heather, clearly delighted at her achievement. 'That means I'm not a boy!'

'But you're a girl,' said Cassie. 'Why do you have to lick your stupid elbow to prove it?'

Heather straightened up, leaned in towards Cassie and stuck her tongue right out before running back to her friends, her pigtails swinging madly behind her. Cassie watched with her heart sinking as her continuing unfathomable weirdness was related to the others.

Heather and her friends stared across at her, giggling and whispering behind their hands. Cassie hated them just as hard as she could. It was bad enough to get this at school but on a Saturday, too?

Jake shuffled along beside her in floppy-eared devotion as she slunk guiltily home to her back yard. Exhausted by the unfair demands of her mother

– which clearly didn't take into consideration the stupidities of other little girls – she lay in the long grass and let the afternoon heat melt away the troubling image of snotty Heather Mackie and her inexplicably humiliating rituals.

As she closed her eyes against the sun, the green and brown blur of the over-run garden faded to an orange haze that warmed her eyelids. Bees bumbled lazily about her, too furry and fat to be anywhere in a hurry. Jake snuffled nearby, his breath ruffling her hair and tickling one ear. Calmed by the soporific heat, Cassie was blissfully happy imagining tying Heather's pigtails over a branch, pouring jam on her and leaving her to the bees.

Unfortunately just as her daydream got to the sticky good bit, she heard her name being called. Cassie scowled, sure that she was being interrupted for something domestic and therefore futile.

The call came again, louder, more insistent and verging on foolish to ignore. Peeved at being hassled she opened her eyes, sat up, brushing the worst of the mess from her dungarees and cursing the petty tribulations of being eight years old.

Truculence personified, she patted the sleeping Jake and hauled herself across the overgrown lawn and up the back steps into the sunlit kitchen, all the while trying to figure out what she'd done wrong this time. She shuffled her feet in the most non-committal way she knew how and wished, not for the first time, that she had a little brother to blame stuff on.

Kath McCullen had to stifle a bubbling laugh at the sight of her daughter. She had no idea what Cassie had been doing all morning but right about now she looked like the blonde root-ball of a recently disinterred pot-plant. Whatever she'd been up to, it meant not leaving an inch of her unmuddied. Kath longed for the day someone would invent a washing machine you could safely put kids in, fully clothed.

'There's a family next door,' she said. 'They have a little girl, looks about your age. Why don't you take a cookie and go say hey?'

Cassie didn't want to go say hey or much else for that matter. She was on her fifth full day of being livid at the neighbours who had erected a wire cover over their garden pond, just when she had spent weeks trying out increasingly disgusting and messy ways to torture the tadpoles. Cassie's resentment had been all-consuming.

After nearly a week of afternoons wasted in a furious sulk in her tree, she'd also been spying on the new little girl who, to Cassie's absolute horror, wore dresses and nice shoes.

Another Heather Mackie, Cassie had assumed, furious with the universe for the unfairness of it all.

Cassie hadn't seen Jen wearing pink yet, but she'd known for sure it would only be a matter of time.

At this new and horrific suggestion of actual contact Cassie pulled her best scowl which, for reasons she still couldn't fathom, never seemed to go far with her mom.

'Take a cookie and go and say hello, Cassandra.'

Being called Cassandra usually meant she'd lost whatever argument she didn't know they were having and worse, it meant that the phrase 'because I said so' couldn't be far behind. With all the sullenness an eight-year-old could muster, she grudgingly accepted both the proffered cookies, making a brief but all-important mental note to keep the larger one for herself. Cassie and her scowl glared up at her mother.

'I think her name is Jennifer-May,' said Kath.

'S'a stupid name,' grumbled Cassie, although she felt a tiny pang of solidarity for her new neighbour. She thought Cassandra was pretty bad, but Jennifer-May was way worse. She mooched back out into the sunlight.

Since the day they'd moved in, Cassie had instantly loved her back garden more than anything in the world and had everything she needed right here. She had long decided that other kids were only tolerable if playing nice meant a better chance of dessert, treats or presents. Little pink girls were ogre food.

Whenever her dad was home he always made sure the front lawn was mowed and neat. Somehow, though, the next ball game always seemed to start before he ever got round to tending the back garden which now wasn't so much overgrown as jungle. Just in case he ever did find the time, however, Cassie had a secret – though entirely unnecessary – list of interference she planned to run if he ever threatened to tame her wonderful wilderness.

Her pride and joy was an ancient crab-apple tree which dominated the south-east corner. Its thick trunk rose four feet in the air before splitting into half a dozen branches which each ran horizontally for a few feet before curling and twisting up in lots of fun ways. What made this tree really special was the one thick solitary branch that parted from the trunk less than a foot off the ground. It extended three times Cassie's length before it bent suddenly upwards and back on itself, like it was trying to tickle the other branches under their arms.

From a distance, Cassie thought it looked just like her grandmother's arthritic hands, only warmer, not as rough and a whole lot less likely to squeeze her face and yell, for the third time, about how much she'd grown. Not so very long ago, Cassie had squeezed her grandma's face right back and told her how much she'd shrunk. Even her dad's roar of laughter hadn't done much towards restoring her TV privileges that week.

From their first day in the new house, though, that tree had been her refuge and sanctuary from all the imagined ills and injustices Cassie suffered, like taking out the trash, eating vegetables and having to be cleaned for presentation to random relatives.

Stretched out on the long, low branch, Cassie schemed about the autonomy age would bring, dreaming of a day when she could have ten hotdogs for breakfast or tie twenty five helium balloons to Jake to see if he would fly, or put an end to the laundry debate by doing the sensible thing and running around naked. Cassie couldn't wait to be a grown-up when all that decision-making and freedom would be hers. She knew no-one would ever tell her what to eat or when to go to bed or what to wear or how to behave, because being a grown-up clearly meant getting everything your own way.

Happily cocooned between stars and soil, Cassie practically nested amongst the worn branches; reading comics, playing, sulking, plotting and brooding, thrilled to have something that leant itself to being a castle, a raft, a whale, horse or dragon, a tower, a submarine, rocket, cave or pirate galleon with just a little imagination, some rope and a big bit of chalk.

Sometimes, she just liked it being a tree, too, and figured if she could have wrapped its huge arms around her and slept, she would have been blissfully happy, but for one small problem.

Despite the tree's chameleon qualities, there came a point every day she had to be coaxed away. Kath spent most evenings pleading with her daughter to eat something, just once, sitting at a table rather than making herself ill stuffing food down her neck whilst draped over a high branch, pretending to be whatever creature she'd read about in a comic that week.

The first time it happened, Cassie had decided she was a sloth. She couldn't believe any animal had such a perfect life, spending eighteen hours a day asleep, somewhere warm or hanging upside down from trees. What followed was one of the most exasperating weeks she had ever put Kath and Mickey through. They had tripped over her curled up and pretending to nap everywhere from a dark kitchen floor at 6 a.m. to inside the laundry basket, the latter nearly causing Kath a coronary when the dirty towels had jumped at her.

What had stopped it all, unfortunately, was the Aye-Aye, another creature which Cassie had read nested in trees but also ran around at night on all fours, making wet clicking noises whenever it was full. At that point, Kath had given up trying to explain their daughter's behaviour to anyone, but she was stuck. Rescinding privileges seemed ludicrous given that bizarre tree-dwellers was what got Cassie reading. Still, she drew the line at leaving Cassie's dinner hidden under rocks or spread along tree branches as requested. Cassie hadn't been amused and out-sulked herself, rendering any kind of negotiation impossible until Kath put chocolate ice-cream in the freezer and waited for her daughter to melt.

Right now, however, Cassie was far too taken with next door's garden and had finally decided that she wasn't going to let inconvenient neighbours get in her way. As soon as breakfast was over every morning, Cassie spied from her tree, waiting till the Hollier family was off the premises. With them gone, she snuck through a convenient hole in the hedge which had only appeared after she'd kicked some particularly tenacious plant-life to death.

Having made it clear to the hedge just who was in charge, she set about bringing doom and destruction to the unsuspecting inhabitants of the pond. It didn't take the tadpoles long to realise survival meant hiding in the murky depths. When Cassie's stick ran out of victims, she took to running between both gardens, indulging her vivid imagination with increasingly complex scenarios. These tended to involve roguish but ultimately terribly decent pirates, princes who came to rescue beautiful princesses (who could rescue themselves thank-you-very-much but why bother when it's so hot?) and handsome jungle explorers whom she saved from hungry cannibals with an exotic combination of ballet and karate-chopping, with added hypnotic singing where necessary.

Whenever Kath checked up from the kitchen window, she found her daughter having an animated though one-sided conversation (with intermittent screeching) whilst arabesquing, hacking leaves off unsuspecting bushes and hurling small rocks at cornered tadpoles, having yet again developed selective deafness at every admonishment to stay in her own garden.

Kath, though delighted at her daughter's wildly creative games, figured there'd be a much happier little girl lording it over the back garden if only she didn't have to rule the world all by herself. Cassie, however, just wanted someone to tie to the tree.

That was all her dad's fault.

During the previous winter when he'd been home for a whole, wonderful week, he'd read her a bedtime story about a bow and arrow and a dumb boy with fruit on his head. She'd ventured into the garden the next day with a plentiful supply of apples but was hindered by the shortage of easily-explained weaponry. Undeterred, she'd decided that small rocks would make a serviceable substitute. In the first place she tried coaxing Jake into sitting still under the tree but a dim, enthusiastic beagle fell short of requirements as neither dog nor apple would stay put.

Her frustration peaked by the time she was considering hurling rocks at a banana resting wonkily atop a snoozing puppy. It was clear she'd strayed too far from the drama of the original tale and it was going to have to be dumb boy and apple or not at all.

In the park the next afternoon she'd approached all the boys she knew but none of them seemed particularly keen. Eventually, and reluctantly, she resorted to the 'come-with-me, I've-something-to-show-you' routine that other girls seemed to pull off pretty easily but Cassie found no takers, possibly as she'd made the earlier mistake of mentioning the rocks. It didn't even occur to her that her many scratches, scabs, bruises and cuts suggested she might be something of a liability.

Cassie, whose friends were all boys, had absolutely no idea how you went about finding a girl to play with and having met Heather Mackie, was pretty sure she never wanted to. In her experience, girls were usually afraid to get dirty and ran away squealing at first sight of a bug. Worse, they played with dolls and fluffy toys and giggled at most everything and kept making kissy faces at boys Cassie was trying to play with. On a sliding scale of fun things to do with your body, Cassie rated kissing somewhere between sneezing and being sick.

And now she was sitting on the low branch of her tree, a cookie in each hand and under orders to make friends. Cassie stared at the hole in her hedge and mourned the loss of her solo playground beyond. Every inch of her eight-year-old being resented having to give a cookie to the traitor who'd stolen her tadpoles.

Even the cookies presented a dilemma. The larger one had one less Smartie than the other but really was much bigger. Cassie loved Smarties and knew which drawer they were hidden in, so figured the bigger cookie was still the better bet. She briefly considered eating the smaller one and fibbing about playing nice. A quick glance at the kitchen window brought a wave from her mother and any thoughts of cheating evaporated. Cassie let out a very long sigh. By the time she looked back at the hole in the hedge, there was a face peeking through the torn branches.

Kath watched the two girls encounter each other for the first time.

'Mickey,' she called over her shoulder, 'come see this,' and a moment later her husband ambled through from the den.

She looked at him. 'Get this,' she said, 'it's like High Noon for kids!'

He slipped his arm around her waist and they watched in silence.

Cassie approached the battered foliage and stood, her head on one side, as the mysterious Jennifer-May stared at the muddy and freckled vision before her who looked, for very good reasons, like she'd been dragged backwards through a hedge. Twice.

Every time Cassie tried to look in her eyes, Jennifer-May's head would bob a little harder until her gaze was so averted she was just staring at her three-buckle, patent black leather shiny shoes.

Cassie had no idea what to do. If this girl had only been a boy she could have introduced herself with a swift kick in the shins or the gift of a dead arm, but this was weird. It wasn't until she looked down again at the clutched cookies that inspiration finally struck. She thrust one towards the stranger and stood amazed as Jennifer-May ran off.

– What kind of idiot doesn't want a cookie? she thought, and absent-mindedly began to munch on it. Realising she'd started the smaller one by mistake, she guiltily glanced up at the back porch, hastily stuffing the bigger cookie in her pocket for later.

In the kitchen, Mickey kissed his wife's cheek.

'Remind you of anyone?' he asked, and, ducking

away from a dishwater-soaked finger, went back to his game.

At another kitchen window, Mary watched the same scene play out, her heart sinking as her daughter slunk into the kitchen, picked up her book and went to her room.

On the third day, and the third set of cookies Cassie had every chance of eating alone, Jennifer-May finally mumbled something inaudible to all but her feet.

'Mmm?' said Cassie.

'Do you want to come play in my garden?' came a whisper.

Cassie was stunned. It simply hadn't occurred to her that the Holliers' arrival didn't mean the garden was lost to her. Now she realised that maybe there was a point to making friends with just this one girl – she could have it back! Maybe not all to herself, but a garden with a girl in it was miles better than no garden at all.

'S'pose,' she conceded but as she went to clamber through the hedge she paused, deciding that momentous things should start off right. She shoved the cookies in her pockets, turned over a stone with her foot and was delighted to find the ground crawling with tiny bugs.

'Look at this,' she said to her new neighbour, utterly thrilled when Jennifer-May crouched down and let the ants crawl over her fingers. 'They tickle,' she flashed a nervous grin up at Cassie.

Cassie reached into her pockets and in a move entirely unprecedented (or surpassed in the years to come) gave the bigger cookie to Jennifer-May. The little girl in the dress accepted the treat and they both ate in silence. Then Jennifer-May took Cassie by surprise with a huge smile.

Cassie stopped mid-munch. She didn't know what to do. Jennifer-May had the kind of smile that made the sunshine feel just that little bit warmer on her skin. It shifted Cassie's world on its axis and Cassie, even if she'd intended to play it cool, couldn't help but smile right back.

Back in her own garden Jen was feeling brave. As the girls sat on the grass she suggested to Cassie a game she loved but which needed two players. She explained how the edges of the lawn were the game boundaries, how they would use fallen sticks to mark out squares and about what moves you were allowed to make, in three directions, always adding up to nine as you tried to get from danger (the dark end of the garden by the shed) to safety (the back porch). It was exciting, she tried to persuade Cassie, because you had to be good at Math, thinking up new patterns all the time. Cassie stroked Jake's ears.

'No. We'll play my game. It's better.'

She took great pains to set the scene for Jennifer-May who'd never heard anything like it, but decided, mostly because she didn't know how to get a word in, that she would be more than happy to let Cassie lead the way.

In the settling dusk, the girls finally got round to using Jennifer-May's back porch as the sole surviving bit of their pirate galleon after an attack by giant squid had left it smashed to smithereens on the edge of a whirlpool. Happily, they found it came equipped with two glasses of home-made lemonade.

Sitting cross-legged in the middle (so that no stray surviving killer tentacle could drag them to a dizzy death), Jennifer-May tried to decide how, when they played again tomorrow, they could make Jake the Killer Beagle look more like a ten-legged monster from the briny deep. She was reasonably sure that Cassie had been kidding about killing and eating any monsters.

An oblivious Jake lay in adoring exhaustion by Cassie, licking her bare feet and generally being far more floppy-eared than any squid either girl had ever seen.

As they were drinking, Mary came outside.

'Cassie,' she said, 'you're always welcome to come

play here. It's so lovely for Jennifer-May to have made a friend.'

Cassie mumbled something that might have been a thank-you for the lemonade, then the girls glanced surreptitiously at each other over their tumblers, saying nothing more until they were alone.

'Only my mom calls me Jennifer-May,' said Jennifer-May.

'My mom only calls me Cassandra when she thinks I've been bad,' volunteered Cassie.

Yet more smiles were exchanged and it had been Cassie and Jen ever since, except when their games took on new dimensions depending which movie they'd been allowed to see. Both sets of parents had to get over the embarrassment of calling Darth Cassie and Indiana Jen in for their supper.

Jen would soon discover that Cassie's games, like her monsters, mutated overnight. For a little girl whose friends were all books, Cassie was Jen's own personal magic wand, weaving three-dimensional wonders from her favourite stories. By the end of the first week of their friendship, Jen had become the owner of a pair of dungarees and the shiny shoes had been unceremoniously dumped for a pair of machine-washable sneakers. It wasn't long before Mary had to consult Kath for advice about how the hell you got grass and oil and mud and tar and the smell of puppy out of denim. They both agreed the unidentifiable stains didn't bear thinking about, although Kath knew smeared frog when she saw it.

# Chapter Four

My childhood was nothing exceptional. I went to school, read books, did pretty much as I was told.

As they contrived endless embarrassing schemes to help me make more friends, I would try explaining to my parents that I preferred just to watch and listen. All in vain. I could sense a scheme from a mile away and at the earliest sign of interference would escape to the library. What parent could legitimately complain their kid reads too much?

But at the end of every visit for ten years I'd leave that library like a crazy person. I'd stand on the very edge of the wide stone step, just listening, my toes tipping into the dip worn by thousands of visitors. Then, still under the lip of the building, I'd crane my neck forward and look up, checking for falling dogs. That was Dog's fault.

See, I knew even then that the stupid over-breed because they have nothing else to occupy their moronic minds. Dog was the most stupid creature I'd ever met so I figured he must come from a pretty huge family. So there must have been parents and the rest of a litter and maybe whatever dumb children he'd fathered before he ever came to end his short idiotic life with us. I reckoned that if all of them were as stupid as Dog, they might have chosen to live in a library because they were too stupid to know they couldn't eat books. Then maybe one day, half-starved and crazy, they'd try to eat one of the pigeons resting on the gutters and I'd get hit on the head by one of Dog's dumb relatives.

To begin with I actually did go there to read but by the time I was in my late teens, I would fall into one of the worn, sagging sofas, drop an open book in my lap and just watch the world through huge, dirty windows. Even back then I liked to watch couples. Always couples. I got good at telling when there was an argument brewing and there was nothing I hated more than them moving out of sight before I had seen it manifest. Now I just follow and watch but back then I was too awkward to be truly inconspicuous.

When couples looked happy, I liked to invent little scenarios for them, fantasising difficult, dangerous and cruel futures that would drive them to despair, disease and an early grave. I always saw their contentment as a lie they thought it was OK to tell the world. I hated being lied to.

The more I watched, the more the lies got to me.

I'd seen so many people behaving in such dumb, petty, mean ways that I couldn't just join in; couldn't play the game. I knew too much. I knew that when it came my turn, things would have to be different.

I didn't check any other buildings. I mean, I really convinced myself there was a danger of a dog falling on me outside the municipal library, but that one thing doesn't make me crazy. I've met people who believe in far weirder things than that.

By my late teens I was really angry watching people my own age fall in and out of what they called love. It wasn't love. How can it be love when someone could just abandon you when they got bored, or things got difficult or they got what they thought was a better offer? That's not an acceptable way to behave. Someone who loves you will stay with you always. I'd read enough books to know that was true. Someone who loves you will be there every single minute of every single day.

See, I already knew how easy it was to be any kind of person. It's no effort, really. If you tell someone who you are, make them really believe you – be really super-convincing – then everything you say and do will be judged in context. You can get away with murder, you know?

Like if you tell someone your dad beat you when you were a kid, you can make them be nicer to you more of the time, so even if you treat them pretty badly, they'll let it go further before they try and make you stop. And they'll even feel bad about doing it, bad enough for both of you. Bad enough so that you don't have to bother.

But what's the point in reinventing yourself if you don't have someone you can prove it to? They have to see everything you do, hear everything you say, feel everything you feel if they are going to be any value at all. People will tell you they're interested or they care, but when it comes down to it, they're not really paying proper attention. If they were, they'd be willing to put their entire life on hold and devote themselves to you. I didn't want anything less than that, do you see?

I couldn't bear the thought that someone might think I was just like everyone else. I knew that when I got involved, it would be special. Different. Better.

So when the time came, I didn't want to waste myself on just any woman. I wanted it to be perfect, right from the start. My ideal woman was out there somewhere and I was willing to wait for her. I knew she'd find me and once she did, she'd stay with me. She'd be my shield against all the lies and pain and danger and unhappiness. I would be hers completely and she would spare me the petty cruelties of the world. People would see us and see our happiness was for real. They would envy not just what we had, but who we were and what we made of each other. That's how it was going to work, I just knew it.

So I kept on watching, but not couples. Just women. I waited to feel something good, something that would tell me they were the one.

But I didn't feel anything, no matter how hard I wanted to. It was like I was empty.

I wanted to see proof of depth and character but it seemed all the women I watched did nothing more than preen like ludicrous tropical birds. They screeched, flashed their feathers, danced around waiting to be noticed, glorying in passing appreciation of their most irrelevant attributes. They pretended to have opinions and feelings when it was clear all they really wanted was to be worshipped. Yet they did nothing to earn it. And what value has worship when offered by scum? It got so bad that all I ever felt was contempt.

Mostly I watched them on dance floors, parading themselves before any man, indiscriminate to the point of insult. And for what? For a free drink? For a moment's attention? All too often, seemingly for no reason, they'd change their mind. I'd watch them relay some guy's most minor flaw to a posse of third-rate breeders who would screech and smirk and mock as if they inhabited some higher moral ground which bestowed on them privilege and immunity.

They were such whores.

I watched, aloof and increasingly bilious with disdain. I found them despicable. My contempt became a hatred, over time. I'd stand in the shadows, always watching, playing through fantasies in my mind in which I liked to cast myself as the redeemer. I imagined I would dance, smile and chat. I would indulge. I would make small flirtatious remarks. I would play the game. The mechanics of these imaginings never really mattered because they all ended when I would present one of these sluts with a cocktail laced with powdered glass and maybe a little of whatever industrial chemical I could find. With that simple act I would have the power to render them both silent and infertile. It seemed the perfect crime. It seems naïve now, but I was 18 and I loved those fantasies. They made me feel calm. I often crave the life that might have been if only I had done it. I regret not doing it. It would have been a mercy. A cleansing.

Still, for all the clubs were filthy, crowded hell-holes, I couldn't keep away. I was seduced by the anonymity of the dark. To be alone, just watching, heightened my escalating sense of removal. It was a comfort, to be separate.

One night I lay awake in our tiny apartment, restless and with a quiet fury building inside me. Every nerve-ending in my body demanded some kind of action; my hands twitched, the skin tingling. I felt as if my veins were in spate, the blood coursing harder and faster through me until I thought my skin might split with the pounding pressure. I felt super-charged, filled with a sudden desire to run at the walls, knowing I would feel no pain. Something had to give. I left the house.

I walked for hours until, taking an unfamiliar route home, I saw three security guys sharing a smoke at the entrance to an alley. As I approached they moved aside, revealing a flight of damp stone steps ending at an open doorway. Picking my way around the junk food litter, the slick grease spots and broken glass, I didn't dare let go of the splintered wooden handrail. As I reached the doorway, the club's pounding bass pulsed through my teeth. Grinding them together, I stepped inside.

The grimy, flickering fluorescent glare of the bar's strip lights hurt my eyes after the dim stairwell and, when I stopped squinting, I endured the moment's attention I warranted from the drinkers nearest the door. Ignoring them, I made my way through the room being careful not to touch anyone, nor allow myself to be touched.

The tunnel-shaped bar opened into what seemed a cavernous room, the walls obscured by the suffocating fog of dry ice which was suffused with an amber glow from ceiling-mounted spotlights. My eyes took time to adjust to the gloom.

In the mist far across the room I began to see people dancing, their outline blurred in the haze, their entire shape black as if the person had been cut from the fabric of the universe and discarded, leaving a hole through which I could see the empty darkness beyond.

Watching them made me thirsty.

This time my entrance to the bar didn't merit even a glance. With the crowd three-deep waiting to be served I stood close to the centre and waited. Looking down, I saw a hand massaging the ass of the woman directly in front of me. I traced the arm to find her boyfriend. They were dressed in his-and-hers versions of the same outfit; both in tight black t-shirts, she in a floor-length black skirt, he in dark jeans one size too small, judging by the paunch straining his belt. Each time he kissed her she cast the quickest glance at me, then pushed herself up against him, arching her back under the slight pressure of his hand as he pulled her to him. They were so close to me I could hear every wet sound of their embrace.

He kissed her with his eyes open as if he needed constant reminding just who she was. Each time she came up for air she flicked her long black hair in an overly theatrical fashion copied from the tackiest shampoo commercials. It keep hitting me in the face and each time I took a soft lashing it made me hate her more because she knew I was right there, yet showing even the slightest consideration was clearly beyond her. Slut.

Every move she made was for an audience. Sometimes she jutted one hip, standing at a forced angle, casting her glance around the bar. Twice for no reason she stretched out one arm, arching her wrist and fingers, only to play with her hair again, whipping it against me.

When her boyfriend briefly turned to look beyond me to the door, it was clear just from his face that he was around ten years her senior – she couldn't have been more than twenty-two – and I was intrigued by the four-inch scar which ran the length of his cheek. It was deep and with just that little glance I could imagine what his face must have looked like when it was done. I pictured the lower jowl, hanging slack with the weight of the gouge, gaping to expose the subsurface tissue, scarlet and raw.

I wondered, too, if his attention-seeking whore ever kissed it? I pictured her sliding the pink tip of her tongue from the deep puckering by his lip to where it petered out past his left eye.

And in that moment I felt truly sorry for him. He was a curiosity to her; a choice to confound friends, parents and future lovers. As age began to show on his face, gravity would distort his scar and what passed as character now would soil him in the future.

From his eyes I knew that he knew. I could almost see him storing, minute by minute, the memory of this shallow, self-serving creature to prove to himself in years to come that there had once been a time when he deserved beauty.

She knew it too, and his gratitude and pawing, fawning devotion clearly drove her.

I wanted her dead.

They turned to leave and she stared at me, looking me up and down. She made the briefest eye contact then slid past, gently pressing herself against me as she went, even though there was plenty of room. I looked away.

It took another ten minutes to be served but once I had my beer I hurried back through to the dance floor, anxious to be made invisible.

I felt myself disappear inside the cloudy dark; my heartbeat slowing as the loathing abated. I sipped my drink, letting my eyes settle on individuals for a few seconds at a time, always trawling, always considering.

Near me, I saw a girl I thought was leaning against the wall, but as I watched I realised that what I had taken to be shadows sliding across her, was actually fingers gently stroking her cheek. She was leaning back against someone. A stranger? Unlikely. Only a boyfriend would make such a tender gesture. Her eyes slowly closed in bliss. Although I began to feel uncomfortable – as if I was intruding – I wished those were my fingers. I imagined how soft and cool her skin must feel, how comforting to have the gentle weight of your beloved against you, hiding you, shielding you.

After a few moments they stood apart, clearly ready to leave but that's when I saw him lean into her and gently take her chin in his hand before sweetly kissing her. They both had their eyes closed.

I swore to myself then that when I found my ideal woman I would stroke her cheek and hold her chin when I kissed her, and anyone witnessing us would see she was exquisite, precious and beautiful by my tenderness.

I needed to see more and so was on the street before them, although I bowed my head and looked away as they walked past.

I followed them for eight blocks. Their arms intertwined, she sometimes laid her head on his shoulder and he kissed her hair, pulling her closer as he did so.

This would be me, one day soon. I let them alone and went home to think.

With rare exceptions like that one couple, clubs seemed to be populated by bitches and predatory Neanderthals and that always made me feel better. It made me feel superior. It reassured me that I was right to aspire to higher things, proving to me over and over again what I had suspected all along, that these were inane, trivial people of little worth, that their lives were inconsequential. It's not so much that they wouldn't be missed, more that it would be doing humanity a favour to remove them from the gene pool. I enjoyed that thought so much, even the music couldn't spoil it for me.

# Chapter Five

Despite being in different classes for their final years of elementary school, the girls were as good as inseparable. Cassie sought out Jen almost every day at break, usually sneaking up behind her and snapping her book closed. Jen's admonishments were invariably addressed to Cassie's back as she was dragged off to join in whatever chaos was, or would soon be in orbit around her best friend. Lunchtimes were different. Cassie would be surrounded by most of the boys in her class, her table always the loudest and messiest, with a reluctant Jen sat on the end, nodding when Cassie needed her to. She wondered why Cassie hung around with these dumb boys who always told lies about how fast or far they could run, or how late they'd stayed up, or what trouble they'd got away with. Jen knew they were lying, but Cassie didn't notice or seem to care.

Still, she loved that Cassie waited by the gate for her at the end of every afternoon so they could walk home together. Jen would quickly do her homework and help Cassie with hers. Then the evening was theirs. The more Jen read, the more she made suggestions to Cassie for games, but it was always Cassie who took Jen's best idea and made it better, wilder, bigger, more exciting and inevitably messier than Jen could ever have imagined.

When they started high school they hung out together every day, at least whenever Jen wasn't in the library or Cassie wasn't in detention. They shopped often, fought rarely and holidayed together; the potential of their respective parents not getting on had never even occurred to them.

Sleep-overs, camps, trips and school outings – when one was going, it was assumed they both were. Kath and Mary got used to doing laundry they didn't recognise, and treating both girls as their own.

No matter which one of them got caught doing something ridiculous or dangerous – building a fire, tasting paint, shoving cheese in the dog's ears – the other always said, 'I told her not to do it.' When one was sick, Dr Brooks would automatically write a line for both. It had been an agreement grudgingly reached after a long and pointless year of one girl skipping school to hide out with the other, getting just as sick and then the other hanging around out of misplaced solidarity. The chickenpox summer had been especially unpleasant.

One December afternoon in their final year of school the only thing on the girls' minds was a serious shopping trip, a movie, pizza and Dairy Queen before curfew. They came bursting through Cassie's front door in a major hurry to get changed, Jen being regaled at volume with Cassie's ever-changing plans for her imminent eighteenth.

Kath was kneeling on the kitchen floor beside Mickey.

'Mom?' Cassie shook Jen's hand off her arm and walked right in and sank down beside her parents.

Kath turned to her and said, 'Your dad's dead. Do something.'

Mickey looked up at Cassie, then, trying to smile. He took her hand. 'I'm OK,' he said, then his eyes rolled back a little and his hand went limp in hers.

Kath kept saying 'Mickey?' over and over, then she started to cry. But it wasn't the quiet kind of crying you do when you feel sorry for yourself. Cassie had never heard either of her parents do anything as uncontrolled as cry, and her mother's howling was a sound that would keep her awake with nightmares for months afterwards. Jen recovered enough to run out the door screaming for her mom.

In the way that neighbourhoods absorb news without being told, there was a concerned and curious crowd waiting in the gathering dusk as paramedics wheeled a breathing but unconscious Mickey McCullen out the door. Mary climbed into the ambulance, helping a dazed Kath up to sit beside her. Cassie went to follow but a paramedic had already started to shut the doors. Kath, as if finally remembering her daughter was there said, 'No. Stay here and look after the house.'

Then the doors were closed and, with sirens blaring, Cassie's dad was taken from her.

Jen tried reaching for Cassie but was pushed roughly aside. Cassie didn't want anyone to touch her. She turned and stared at the assembled crowd, her eyes streaming, her chest heaving, then she ran back inside her own house, slammed the door and threw herself down on the still-warm kitchen floor where she stayed for hours until she had screamed herself hoarse.

Choking and sobbing, convinced she'd never see him again, she lay where he had lain until the floor was cold, then she went through to their liquor cabinet and fetched a nearly full bottle of Scotch.

Jen's dad John led her firmly home, insisting quietly that Cassie would be fine but promising that he would go check on her in a little while. Jen switched on the TV and slumped on the sofa, leaning against her dad, staring past the flickering screen at Cassie's kitchen window. John put his arm around her and she swivelled round, laying her feet across his lap and curling into his shoulder. They were dozing together like that four hours later when Mary phoned.

A little before midnight, Mary parked in her own drive then walked across both front lawns and let herself in to Kath's house, feeling like an unwelcome guest. The silence was as wrong as waking at 4 a.m. when, having listened for an intruder, what you can't hear is somehow more frightening. Mary stood in the moonlit hall letting her eyes adjust to the near dark and chastising herself for being spooked by the quiet.

Walking into the kitchen, she flicked the light switch and gasped when she saw Cassie propped in a corner. The girl's arms were caked in blood and there was broken china scattered across the floor.

Cassie's face, arms and legs were daubed with dried dark smears and livid welts. Her clothes were torn and stained where she'd thrown up. The empty bottle lay near one hand and if it hadn't been for the small spasms pulsing through Cassie's fingers, Mary would have thought her dead.

Gagging on the smell of stale vomit, Mary opened a window then took a small brush and swept most of the smashed crockery to the other side of the room. With shaking hands she ran a bowl of warm water then sat on the floor before Cassie with a clean dish-cloth. She started to wipe softly at the blood, feeling for shards of china as she went, trying as gently as possible to find out just how much damage had been done.

Cassie's eyelids fluttered.

'Cassie, angel, it's Jen's mom, Mary. You've cut yourself pretty badly. I'm just trying to clean you up, OK?'

Cassie only stared through heavy-lidded red eyes as a string of drool ran from the corner of her slumped mouth.

'Cassie, I need you to tell me if you took anything else with the Scotch. Can you do that, honey? Please, it's important. Did you take any pills?'

Cassie shook her head, just a little, then started to cry.

'Where's my dad?'

Mary stopped what she was doing, staring down at her hands. Since she'd left Kath with her mother across town she'd tried all the way home to figure out a way to say this but nothing had seemed right.

Cassie's voice rose in pitch and she tried to move.

'I want my dad.'

'Cassie, I'm so sorry…'

As if she'd been electrocuted, Cassie's body went

into spasm, kicking Mary in the gut and winding her. As Mary struggled to clear some space around the girl, Cassie seemed unable to stop twitching all over until she finally stretched her neck, half-turned herself and threw up again. For nearly twenty minutes, distress tore the breath from her in choked gasps as her ragged breathing was punctuated with fierce retching and asthmatic wheezing.

Eventually, Mary got her to take some Valium she found in the bathroom cabinet and, with Cassie sedated, dressed the worst of her wounds. She washed the girl and wrapped a bath robe around her, then wriggled close to her and held her, hoping just the warmth and heartbeat of another human being might help calm her.

With dawn showing on the horizon, Mary remained with Cassie leaning against her shoulder, softly running her fingers through the girl's hair.

'Oh Cassie,' she whispered, looking at her bandaged arms, 'why?'

In the half-dark room she heard a doped voice, lost and broken, whisper, 'I had to let the hurt out.'

Not for the first time that night, Mary cried, wishing there was something worth saying.

Early in the morning she put a half-conscious Cassie to bed. They were soon joined by Jen who sat in the room fretting and feeling redundant. After a little while, not knowing what else to do, she slipped off her shoes and climbed onto the covers to curl up around her best friend, holding her close.

Leaving the two girls alone, Mary went home and let John silently fold his arms around her. None of the things that had been in her head all night would form themselves into coherent words. Every morning when she kissed him goodbye she always expected he'd be coming home. She knew where he was, what he was doing, could picture his train, his office, his colleagues. The idea that one day he might not come back was more than she could bear.

Later in the day they rifled through the attic, eventually unearthing an unused wedding present dinner service which she took next door and stacked in Kath's cupboards. She checked on the girls who were both asleep, then she and John sat down to go through their finances and see what they could spare to help out. Without being asked, John called his boss and, after explaining the situation, got permission to take a week's leave. For the rest of the day and indeed the week they were inseparable. Mary needed to be able to see and touch him all the time and John was happy to be clung to.

Kath came home a few days later and for months she and Cassie seemed caught in slow motion, immobilised with grief, barely registering day or night.

Kath's family came and went, Mary helped when she could, but their little corner of the world seemed to have ground to a halt. Jen watched over Cassie in silence, reading in a corner, waiting to be useful. Cassie barely talked or ate and seemed to sleep most of the time. Around the first anniversary, she seemed unable to breathe without retching and it fell to Jen to proffer paper bags to help her breathe freely.

As Summer warmed skin and land, movement gradually returned to the McCullen house. In the midst of a redecorating frenzy, Kath took a delivery at home one afternoon and later appeared on Mary's doorstep with a box of carefully wrapped china.

Over coffee, at Kath's prompting, Mary gave a heavily edited explanation of what had happened the night of Mickey's collapse trying, unconvincingly, to make it sound as if any damage Cassie had done had been accidental. Kath had just nodded, eventually made her excuses and gone home.

When Kath had found Mickey all she wanted was her own mother to take charge, tell her what to do, tell her everything would be all right. Instead she'd felt her mind freeze over. Mickey was on the floor. But Mickey danced. Mickey ran. Mickey cooked and climbed and built toys for Cassie. Why was Mickey on the floor? She doesn't know how long she sat with him, but she remembers being grateful to see Cassie, because now someone else would take charge. Someone else would know just what to do and everything would be taken care of.

She tries hard to believe that she did what she thought was right but knows that she'd not really been thinking.

She remembers getting into the ambulance and thinking, with sudden clarity, that Mickey was hers and hers alone. He had been hers since they'd first met, aged ten, in a classroom when she was the first to smile at the awkward new kid. He had walked her home that afternoon, carrying her books. On her front lawn she had kissed him on the cheek and run inside and when she peeked from her bedroom window five minutes later, Mickey was still standing on the grass, grinning.

That summer had been one of holding hands and innocent kisses, of campfires and tree-houses, of gifts and secret codes.

They had made forever promises to each other by the lake. Kath and Mickey, together forever. Back when Mickey loved only her.

As much as she wants to, she feels no guilt for leaving Cassie behind the night of Mickey's collapse but dreads the subject ever being raised. Kath knows that she will never be able to explain to her daughter why – in that split second as the doors were being closed – she felt such resentment for the little girl who had stolen a heart she thought was all hers.

The very worst of it is that in the early hours, Mickey had regained consciousness for a few glorious minutes, and although he'd taken her hand, the only speech he'd managed was to ask after Cassie. Kath hadn't known what to say. She'd stroked his fingers and said, 'She's fine,' but was spared having to explain any further as that's when Mickey had died.

Later that night, Kath snuck into Cassie's room and softly pulled back the duvet. She sank to her knees at the edge of her daughter's bed, clutching the corner of the comforter to her mouth to muffle the cry that escaped her. She stared, utterly horrified as the light from the hall illuminated the random scarring and deep, dark shadows that littered her daughter's limbs.

She gently replaced the cover and went to bed, hugging herself and crying quietly in the dark. She wished more than anything that she could just have asked Cassie to show her the wounds, but on top of everything else, she didn't feel anywhere near strong enough to withstand the accusatory bickering that too many of their encounters now seemed to become.

Their most recent fight had become a screaming match, both women incoherent with fury. It hadn't been about anything in particular, but had escalated from their joint inability to maintain the façade of a daily life and Cassie's unerring ability to wind her mother up simply because she could. The episode had ended worse than usual with Cassie storming out, but stopping in the open doorway where she turned to Kath and with a venomous glare, hissed, 'I lost the wrong fucking parent.'

It would be ten years before she would apologise.

After the initial shock of losing her dad, Cassie couldn't have been less approachable if she'd worn spiked armour and spat boiling oil at anyone within reach. Jen was the only person that she could bear to have around, even if it was only to ignore her. Jen was fine with that. She felt important being the buffer between Cassie and the world, utterly content to read magazines or doze or watch quiet TV while Cassie slept, and would sit and brush her best friend's hair as she lay, staring into space sometimes for hours on end, little more than catatonic.

While in the Fall Jen started her Environmental Studies course as planned, Cassie had been given special dispensation by Ryerson to wait until the second semester to join her photography course. Her concentration wasn't so much depleted as verging on chronic ADD, and having been so keen on college, she now seemed determined to remain in a state of oblivious apathy which extended to everything from her appetite to her counselling.

Near-crippled with her loss, Cassie made a conscious decision to back into a safe, dark corner in her mind where nothing would ever be able to sneak up on her and she'd always see danger coming long before it could even think of hurting her.

She found breathing difficult, not least because she'd run out of reasons to do it.

Unable to sleep unless it was light outside, initially her nights were spent huddled in a corner of her room, afraid of every shadow and noise and keening for her dad. He had been her protection and now he was gone. She'd never had to worry about what was out there that might hurt her because he was always between her and whatever it was. Now she was exposed and vulnerable, open to attack like wriggling bait in a trap. The only answer was to become quiet and still, to become invisible.

She felt like the tiniest of a set of Russian Dolls, as if all the other dolls had been pulled apart, layers stripped away, until the smallest had been replaced inside the largest. All the protection discarded, she felt dwarfed by herself. The smallest one should have been the one that didn't come apart. The smallest one should have been the one that believed in summer forever and true love and magic and happy ever after. Cassie didn't know how to feel like that any more.

In that cocooned state she could see the person that resembled Cassie, see her eat and sleep and drink and cry and dream and walk, but had forgotten how to exert control over any of it. She felt like the very core of herself, this tiny, powerless creature, was trapped, rattling around inside some horrendous marionette, some mockery of her, a demonic, maniacal creature. She became a lie.

As sole breadwinner, Kath had little choice but to move on. She credited her counsellor Gillian with keeping her sane and helping her to begin, after nearly two years, to find time and enough enthusiasm to do things Kath did, not things that Kath did without Mickey. But her daughter proved another matter. Where there had once been a dynamic girl – energetic, vivacious and ready to challenge the world – there was now a shadow; unfocused and shy around strangers. Cassie seemed unwilling to rejoin a world that could do such unwarranted and unexpected damage. She had a desperate need to grow, to occupy the space inside herself again, but that thought brought dread of coming ever closer to the outside world.

On the day she woke feeling excited about the prospect of college she realised, as she got out of bed, that it had been five whole minutes since she'd thought about her dad. The guilt knocked her off her feet and she slid to the floor, weeping uncontrollably, curled into a tight ball, her nails raking the tender skin on her arms, raising scarlet welts. Through her tears she apologised over and over to him, begging his forgiveness.

She made him a promise there and then that he would be the first thing she thought about every morning and the last every night. It seemed like such a simple way to book-end the time she was forced to join the world, and by keeping true to this she began to allow herself to think of other things in the dragging hours between.

In preparation for school, the only books she could be convinced to read were ones she already knew because she knew how they ended.

What scared her more than anything was that someone you loved so completely could leave you and when they did, they took a part of you with them. You could never have it back. It left you with no choice but to live the rest of your life depleted. She knew for certain now that people would abandon her time and again and each departure would leave her a little more demolished.

It was better then, Cassie figured, to keep a reserve, a part of you that wasn't available to anyone. You could store it so far inside yourself that no-one would ever know it was there. A bit of you that could never be taken; a plug so that you could never be completely drained away. All you had to do was build such a strong wall around it that no matter how devastating something was, no matter how hard someone tried to hurt you, you'd always have a piece of yourself intact so you could start over.

She wasn't mad at her dad for leaving, but she knew that in a box in the ground, cold and dead and decomposing, was a part of her.

A month after the horrific fight, Kath and Cassie found themselves having a civil conversation about college over breakfast. Both were feeling their way round the invisible trigger that would shatter the fragile peace.

'I'm thinking of finding an access course to get my Masters,' said Kath, studiously buttering some toast. 'You think it's a good idea?'

Glancing up, all Kath merited was a non-committal shrug, but inside, the real Cassie was thrilled. Having postponed her course a second time, she was tired of reading her course books in secret and tired of feeling guilty about wishing the time away until she could start. The house still gave her nightmares and she'd taken to finding increasingly elaborate ways to get Jen to come home with her whenever she'd ventured out, orchestrating their arrival so she wouldn't have to walk through the door first. Getting out the house seemed like being allowed to stretch after a six-month long-haul flight.

'Sure, mom, why not?'

'I mean, with you gone every day, it would do me the world of good to get the old grey matter moving, I think. Not that I've had to study for an exam in nearly twenty years!'

There it was. Mutual permission to live. Cassie raised a watery smile for her mom then excused herself and took her coffee upstairs where she sat down at her desk, then got up again to make sure her bedroom door was locked. Kath, hearing the click, went out to the back garden, hoping to catch Mary for a chat.

Mary, seeing her friend's feet through the hedge, got up with a groan from weeding and ambled over, only to find Kath failing to keep her tears in check.

'We did it,' she managed, 'we had a whole conversation, at least three minutes, with no shouting or sulking or storming out the room.'

Mary smiled gently and waited for the rest.

'I think she might really go, you know? I was so afraid she'd keep postponing till they would cancel her place, but really I think it's gonna be OK. Trouble is, my half of the bargain is that I'll pick up where I left off. Mickey always said I should.'

Her voice shook a little at the mention of his name, but her eyes found Mary's and she smiled.

While the women chatted, Cassie stood at her window, watching them through a tiny gap in the curtains. She sipped her coffee then crossed the dark room to her desk and switched on the study lamp. Opening the drawer she lifted out some old magazines and from underneath took the letter from the Admissions Office which only required her signature to signal she was ready.

From its leather box on the desk she took the silver pen her dad had given her for Christmas when she was sixteen and, with a whisper to him, signed the form.

# Chapter Six

Only silence and blood have ever made me calm.

I began to go to extraordinary lengths to avoid being with people. Sure, the contempt I felt for them made me feel powerful but it also fed the growing abhorrence I had for any kind of physical contact I had not initiated or approved. Each time there was another brushing against me, or someone's breath on my skin, the anger it raised in me was a tease, mocking my inability to exert control.

Yet all the loathing I felt for those…those oxygen thieves…would dissipate in solitude and silence. My bile fuelled me and every destructive impulse would disintegrate without it.

See, I always liked the kind of peace when it sounded as if the world had been gagged; the cacophony smothered. That was the kind of silence I heard inside me, but it wasn't really silence. Whenever I felt it growing, pushing against my skin, impatient for release, I was afraid to breathe. I knew I couldn't so much as utter a sound because if I just opened my mouth, the silence would reveal itself to be the scream that always ricocheted off my bones. It would break loose and I would be unable to stop it. I would be locked into its fury. That destructive howl would be only the very beginning of what waited for even the smallest chance to burst forth. Fuelled by resentment, it seethed in the dark, waiting for me to start something that couldn't be stopped. I should have been afraid of it, but its wrath was my life force. I took real pride in the mental strength I cultivated that saw each day end without incident.

In those moments my only faith was in the blade. What was blurred became clear; what was turmoil became calm. From the quieted corners of my mind I would watch myself bleed, clot and heal. I loved those little moments of focus…the total clarity as the fog lifted. And all this control from a simple scalpel.

I knew that one day all my waiting, all my sacrifice, would be justified. The right woman would find me and together we would rise above the great unwashed and be more pure, more deserving than any of them. We promised greatness. They were just waiting to die.

But not me. My thighs, my arms, they were testament to my patience. Nothing gave me greater satisfaction than to watch languid rivers of blood crest the puckered scarring as I added one more day's restraint to my tolerant flesh. Like an inmate scratching five-bar gates on a wall, I bided my time with lacerations, the faded lesions a constant reminder of my goal.

# Chapter Seven

With a growing craving for financial independence, Cassie reluctantly took a weekend job assisting a wedding photographer with hours as erratic as the nuptials themselves. The next few months saw her dream of being the next Annie Leibovitz dissolving in a mire of dizzy brides and warring families.

Whenever her boss caught her scowling at work, he would smile vacantly at her and remind her that one day she wouldn't be so scathing about marriage, that one day she would be the princess with her very own Prince Charming. Each time he said it, Cassie would snort and walk away, furious about what a farce the whole thing was and knowing she would never be so tragic as to go through with the whole ludicrous charade. She hated weddings. She would stand by her boss, passing over various bits of equipment and muttering caustic obscenities under her breath at the assembled guests.

Cassie had seen enough taffeta and pastels to do her a lifetime.

All the pictures the families never wanted to see
– the ones that she would have been fired for taking
– now festooned one entire wall of her bedroom.

Her favourites were a near-unconscious drunk
bride half-fallen out her limo door and vomiting
on her driver's shoes; a groom with a bleeding nose
offering one of his usher's teeth back to him and a
garden full of guests tumbling out of chairs that were
sinking into a freshly-watered lawn. She had ceremo-
nially burned the negatives from the fairy-themed
wedding, telling Jen she could take pretty much anything, but 'not that pixie shit' and she figured she
deserved a medal for not kicking a child who once
sat on the floor near her feet and blew his nose on her
only skirt.

With Jen's coursework offering endless opportunities
for volunteering on department projects, the girls saw
little of each other. Cassie began to spend more and
more time in her dark-room, a growing emptiness
inside her fuelled by a world full of image, not experience. As something to hide behind, her camera had
quickly become her protector. It went everywhere
with her, her perfect excuse to observe rather than
participate.

One Saturday in early October, Cassie awoke
with the distilled version of a foul mood that had

settled on her late the night before. She nurtured it throughout the morning, getting increasingly spiky, even by her standards.

Having barely touched her lunch she sat slumped at the table, staring into the middle distance and fuming, her body rigid; nails digging into her palms. When pushed, she had growled at Kath, 'It's nothing to do with dad, it's just…' then jammed her chair back with a screech of protest from the kitchen tiles and stormed off to her room, only feeling a little bad when the door slammed a great deal harder than she'd intended.

Truth was, Cassie had no idea what was wrong, there was just something catching in her world, like going through an entire day trying to remember the one thing that you absolutely weren't supposed to forget to do.

Jen wasn't due home till seven so she went out.

When Jen got home much later than expected she was met at the door by her mom, anxious and demanding to know if she'd spoken to Cassie during the day. Jen told Mary not to worry, that Cassie was probably on assignment, but the news that she had a day off made her suspicious. Cassie rarely did anything without Jen and an unannounced disappearance was unlike her.

By ten, Jen's fretting was verging on panic as

she'd spent the evening wandering to each of their usual hangouts calling for her best friend, even though she knew instinctively it was a fruitless search. For a long time she sat alone on the grass beneath the Girl on a Swing billboard, staring at the traffic speeding by and calmed by the intermittent gentle creaking of the swing. After a while she gave up checking every car that pulled into the lot behind her and headed back. For her, being out past curfew at midnight was unthinkable. As she made her way home, Kath was offloading her anger at Mary, livid at how damn selfish and insensitive Cassie could be, assuming nothing terrible had happened – this was Cassie and chances were she was just suiting herself, as always. That didn't stop both mothers eventually quietly admitting their fears to each other when they thought Jen wasn't listening.

John drove round the neighbourhood checking every corner for the girl but she was nowhere to be found. The cops were called but when they came they asked Jen too many questions. No, they hadn't had a fight. No she didn't know Cassie's boyfriend or if they had a secret place they sometimes went? The cop kept trying to be Jen's friend, pretending he was cooler than her parents, that he just wanted to help. It didn't wash. Something had shifted in Jen's world and even though she didn't have the words to articulate, she knew in her heart that Cassie wasn't dead or in any danger.

After the cop left, Jen sat hugged into a hunch on Cassie's front porch, angrily certain that Cassie was wherever the hell she wanted to be. That thought took her by surprise and she found herself crying, unable to stop.

She couldn't remember a day without Cassie in twelve years. Cassie who had all the best ideas; Cassie who was brave and bright and strong and reshaped the world for them both. Cassie who wasn't afraid of anything or intimidated by anyone; Cassie who could conjure an adventure, a laugh, a risk from thin air. Cassie who knew all the gossip. Cassie who told her everything – everything! – appeared to have run off with a boy Jen knew nothing about. What if she never came back? What if (and just the thought made Jen cry even harder) Cassie was gone for ever? The more upset Jen got, the more she blamed herself. It was because she was boring. Because she never had any good ideas. Because she was too quiet and had been so busy with her course she must have been such a drag this last year.

Jen cried and cried until self-pity finally transmuted to irritation at Cassie for upsetting her. Again. And for the first time ever, resentment flooded through her. How could a boy be more important than her?

How long had Cassie known him? Why didn't she tell her? Why the hell couldn't Cassie be friends with her and have a boyfriend too? The last of her tears dried and Jen felt a bitterness fill her. In the dark with just the crickets for company, she became still and quiet. She'd been rejected. Dumped and abandoned. Cassie had obviously only pretended to be her friend all this time, just whiling away her life until she could run off with some stupid guy.

Jen's anger made her calm.

She remembered Cassie telling her in the months after her dad died that if you loved someone, truly loved them, you willingly gave them part of your heart, glad to be a part of them and you did it without knowing you had handed away a piece of you. At the time, Jen had assumed that Cassie was talking about their friendship a little bit too, but now she knew that wasn't true.

Jen loved Cassie and she would have done anything for her, but this wasn't how best friends were supposed to behave. Jen had given her friendship willingly, trusted Cassie implicitly, loved her unconditionally and had assumed all along that their bond was mutual. As she sat alone in the summer dark, she felt like Cassie was somewhere, mocking her naivety.

'You own a part of me,' she thought, 'so if you

ever need anything from me, you can get it easily enough. You can't have any more.'

Jen asked Kath's permission and in the early hours curled up in Cassie's bed, rocking herself to sleep with the sweet smell of Cassie from the pillow. She dreamed of a stretch of coast they'd all once holidayed on, where summer sun baked the clay hard and an apathetic tide slid thin waves over the ground, turning it gloopy and slick.

In her dream she was all alone, wearing a bathing costume and long t-shirt, walking on warm, soft grass and wet clay, feeling sun on her skin and oily mud between her toes. Soon she found herself indoors, standing in a room where dusty empty boxes were stacked against each wall. An old man with his back to her was intently examining faded writing on each box as she took in the rest of the room. There was only one small, high, barred window, through which streamed sunshine, the split rays illuminating filthy air and falling on a pale marble altar in the middle of the room, over which a white sheet was laid. There was something under the sheet. Curious, though not afraid, Jen stepped forward and pulled the sheet back, revealing her own corpse.

She woke with a start, sucking air into her lungs and trying to draw one full breath. As she lay listening to her hammering heartbeat settle and watching the dawn sky pale, she heard an engine softly idling in the street. Then suddenly a still-drunk Cassie clambered in her own bedroom window.

Before dozing off, Jen had lain in a half-conscious state, running a dozen scenarios through her mind, her favourite being the one where Cassie came crawling back, full of apologies, telling her how special she was, how much she needed her, how she would never let a boy come between them ever again. Magnanimously, she would forgive Cassie and make everything all right. But in her heart Jen knew that Cassie's running off meant, in no uncertain terms, her job was to mop up, to be her audience and confessor, but never her accomplice. That kind of dismissal took a lot of forgiving, more than Jen believed herself capable of or willing to do.

Now she found herself torn between utter relief that Cassie wasn't dead and wishing she'd been found floating face-down in a pond full of vengeful tadpoles. At least if Cassie had summoned the decency to turn up dead Jen could have worn black and publicly mourned their friendship, her grief on full display, but she admitted to herself that she would settle for Cassie being sorry. Very, very sorry.

Hearing Cassie's drunken curses as she fell into the room, Jen knew if she was caught awake she would be expected to hear second-hand of the adventure, be regaled with exaggerations about guys and drink and chaos and then would have little choice but to forgive Cassie, whatever damage had been done at home. But not yet. Jen closed her eyes, slowed her breathing and feigned sleep, hoping Cassie wouldn't check too closely to see if she was faking.

It was very quiet in the room and in the dusky light, Jen opened one eye in time to see Cassie shuck out of her grass-stained clothes down to her underwear, stumbling as she failed to stand on one leg. She fell on the bed.

'Ooof! Sorry, babe,' she muttered, utterly unsurprised to find Jen there, simply climbing in alongside, wriggling until she'd regained possession of most of the single mattress.

The angry confusion within Jen was suddenly rendered weak like a wave pulled back by the undertow. She lay still until Cassie started to snore then opened her eyes, blinking tears away. She could smell summer lawn on Cassie's skin and nestled her nose into her hair, gently resting it against the cool, soft down of her friend's back. She wished Cassie would flip over, throw an arm over her and pull her close, hold her and tell her everything would be OK.

Instead Jen lay in frustrated misery knowing nothing she could or would ever do or say would make any difference. She was jealous and relegated, a position that came all too easily to her in the years to come.

By morning, Kath had reported to both a relieved Mary and an unfazed cop that the girl was home and safe. Later, Jen had stayed in Cassie's room listening to the murmur of voices downstairs, then the shouting, the slammed door that made the house vibrate and the unmistakable sound of a chastised, indignant and grounded Cassie storming back up the stairs to her refuge.

In the relative calm of the bedroom, Jen knew her heartbreak was wasted on Cassie (it had started to feel a little theatrical in the light of a new day), but she was still mad and said as much.

Unrepentant in the face of Jen's muted fury, Cassie simply shrugged at her, flinging herself face down on the bed and pretending to read a magazine. Jen tried to voice her hurt and anger but the threat of yet more tears kept getting in the way and eventually she stopped to take a very deep breath.

'What was the matter, Cassie? Weren't you getting enough attention?'

The room was silent and all Jen could hear was her own ragged breathing. Cassie didn't move. Jen waited until she felt she could speak calmly, though even then her voice was barely more than a whisper when she said, 'I hate you.'

Shaking and nauseous, Jen went home, closing the bedroom door softly behind her. On the bed, Cassie's hands were trembling so badly she accidentally tore the page she was holding. Flinging the magazine across the room, she watched in horror as it bounced off her dresser mirror, knocking a bottle of perfume Jen had bought her the previous week onto the wooden floor where it smashed, releasing a cloud of scent into the small room. Cassie stared at the shattered glass, angry and shamed, then pulled the duvet up around her and wept.

She'd had a horrible night. Some idiot jock she knew from school had got her drunk (not that she'd said no), then taken her to a college party till so far past her curfew she'd figured, vaguely, she might as well just stay out and have as much fun as possible. She remembered telling him that and getting in his car, then next she knew they were on a secluded hilltop on the other side of town where they'd parked and she'd forgotten to say no to a whole bunch of other stuff too.

Now she was bruised and hungover, sore and sick at the recollection that safe sex hadn't graduated to more than a passing thought. She'd wanted to ask Jen to help her find a pharmacy away from the neighbourhood to get a test done, but now that option was gone. She wanted more than anything for Jen to hold her, tell her it was going to be OK, tell her she'd been silly but not so stupid, not really, that these things happened, that boys were rubbish, that she'd always look after her.

Both girls lay in their respective beds, crying and dozing their way through an unbearable day. Neither one ate lunch or supper and a dead quiet settled on both houses. Kath and Mary exchanged quiet words over the hedge, but for all concerned the sun wouldn't set quickly enough.

The following morning, the appearance of normality was restored, but for Jen and Cassie it was months before their storm-struck relationship settled.

When, two years later, Jen got her heart broken by a guy for the first time, she reflected – as Cassie waxed lyrical about how rubbish boys were and how your friends were forever – that being dismissed and abandoned a second time was easier since Cassie had taught her how to survive such an emotional kicking. Even Cassie's hypocrisy didn't really hurt.

As Cassie comforted her ('I'll always be there for you', she said), the tears Jen cried weren't for a meaningless lost boyfriend but for a first love long lost.

# Chapter Eight

I'm ready.

In truth, I've been ready for a long time but it has taken longer than I thought for the perfect woman to find me. I never figured I would have to develop such patience, but I've learned to deal with it. The anticipation, the frustration has, over time, become the good kind of agony. It's important to know when it's the good kind.

Also, I'm not afraid of pain. Pain is the price you have to be willing to pay for something you deserve and I think most times you have to pay up front. It has taken me a long time to figure that out. For too long I'd been unable to tell the bad from good with pain, so my head hadn't always been a good place to be. I endured too much unhappiness and dissatisfaction but inside every wound I found clarity.

In all my time alone, while I waited, I was totally ready, totally willing to be found by my ideal woman; my soul-mate.

I knew that I would know her when she smiled at me. It would be her smile that would tell me she was the one.

There were some women I'd seen whose smile made me forget what day of the week it was; made me stumble over what I was going to say. It was like someone shining a big spotlight on me. I loved that.

I don't even remember how it happened, only one day she wasn't there and the next she was.

With her around, I knew I'd never have to worry about anything or feel bad or alone ever again. I went to see her every day, just to watch, to drink her in.

I had dreamt of her for so long. In all my time alone, I guess I was already in love with the idea of her. Her taste in music, her politics, her dress sense, humour, looks – everything about her would be just right.

I knew she would always be with me, the whole time. I would never want for anything.

I wanted so badly for her to see all the sacrifices I made as I'd saved so much of myself up for her. I knew I could trust her, share this part of me with her because this wonderful woman would be with me forever.

As soon as she was a part of my life I started to feel a little foolish about all the time and energy I'd wasted worrying. See, even when I was without her, she was always one day closer to being with me. I should have doubted less.

I couldn't wait to shop for her; I'd know just what things she'd like. I wanted to cook for her, knowing just what her favourite meal would be. Now when I heard music I could always hear her sweet voice singing along. Paradise would be to fall asleep feeling her warmth near me.

Shauna.

See, my mother always said, 'I want doesn't get.'

Well, Shauna proved her wrong. I wanted her, I waited for her and I deserved her.

Shauna would be mine alone forever and I felt a positive energy surging through me, telling me that all my waiting, my longing, all my sacrifice had been rewarded. I had known all along that I was destined for something great, something special.

With Shauna there was focus and direction in my world.

I didn't have to worry about anything any more because she was going to fix all the little things wrong with my life. She brought clarity to my existence.

There would be no physical, emotional, spiritual or mental burden I couldn't bear so long as Shauna shared it with me.

She would heal me. She would make me complete.

But then, my mother also said, 'You get what you deserve.'

# Chapter Nine

Cassie was finally settling in to life at Ryerson, and although a little over a year behind Jen in her studies, they still saw each other, but only when Cassie wasn't revelling in her new-found freedom.

She hadn't just been ready to start study, she'd been more than ready to get out the house and was quick to take up an offer of a room in an apartment complex near the campus. Jen, however, stayed home, lured by free laundry and a stocked fridge.

Settled in their courses, both were having polar opposite experiences. Cassie partied her way through, glibly riding out her studies on something that was part natural talent and part devil's luck. Jen, however, delighted in a crippling workload that allowed her to regularly claim to be too busy for a boyfriend. It became her standard response every time her mother or grandmother or Cassie (or her aunts, Gita the school secretary, her hairdresser and countless others) saw fit to interfere.

Cassie, oblivious to the hypocrisy, was forever

doling out relationship advice. Overcome with resentment, Jen had on one occasion been feeling brave enough to point out to an oddly quiet Cassie just how unqualified she was to dish it out given that her idea of deep and meaningful meant breakfast the morning after. Her timing had been awful.

An hour earlier, Cassie had been having coffee with her mother, only to find herself under scrutiny before her first full caffeine hit of the day. Kath, expecting to meet two people for breakfast, had bemoaned her daughter's total inability to keep a man around long enough for her to be introduced. Cassie had retaliated with uncharacteristic venom, snapping, 'OK mom, I'll get a boyfriend if you do.'

The pain and loss that swept across her mom's face left Cassie flooded with shame and she'd opened her mouth to apologise but nothing would come. In the appalling silence that followed, Kath swallowed hard and in a small and controlled voice said, 'I know how short a life it can be, Cassie. I just want you to be happy. Don't hate me for that.'

When an unsuspecting Jen added her criticism to Cassie's day it provoked a full-on freak-out with Cassie making it abundantly clear to Jen and every other customer in the diner that no-one was entitled to an opinion on anything she said, thought or did.

A week later when Cassie demanded to be driven

to a pharmacy on the other side of town, the entire trip passed in stony silence with Jen equally disappointed and furious at Cassie's irresponsibility.

Cassie was shrugging off the tail-end of a cold and had snivelled all the way there and back, adding tissues to the crumpled pile accumulating at her feet. The only time Jen spoke to her was to say, 'You know you're really fucking lucky a cold's the worst thing you've caught.'

Cassie sniffed hard and stared out the side window. As long as her immune system still appeared to work she could take any of Jen's feeble jibes.

Jen's revenge for keeping quiet while listening to Cassie pine for the perfect relationship (although over so many men she lost count) was to buy her a little silver bell for her twenty-first birthday. It was meant to be a joke.

Cassie had opened the jewellery box and sat staring at the contents before looking up with a puzzled and curious gaze. 'It's beautiful, babe,' she said, 'but you got me. Why a bell?'

'Pavlov,' said Jen, trying to keep a straight face. 'Nobel Prize winner. Did lots of research into conditioning. He used auditory stimuli when feeding dogs, seeing that they would drool when he rang a bell at feeding time,' Jen grinned at Cassie. 'But he proved with repetition that the dogs would eventually drool at just the sound of the bell, even if they weren't hungry or couldn't see food.'

Cassie wasn't looking any the wiser, and Jen realised as she was talking that while she'd bought the thing as a joke, she had really meant something else.

'You think I'm a dog!' Cassie finally squealed, missing the point entirely, but Jen interrupted the breath being drawn to abuse her.

'No babe, I just figure, you know, that maybe if you can learn to skip straight to the morning after without the night before, I won't lose a lifetime of Saturdays hanging around a pharmacy watching you indulge your legal right to a quick-fix hormone overdose. I'm just trying to get your drooling under control.'

It had been one of their more spectacular fights. Jen lost only a little hair before her mom tried to force them apart. Before she could separate the two, however, Cassie found herself in the wrong place at the wrong time with Jen chucking a lucky punch, and so she spent a week nursing a bruise down one side of her face that went all the colours of a truck-stop oil-slick rainbow.

Jen realised in the aftermath of the scuffle just how tired she really was with Cassie. She wasn't sure she could call their relationship a friendship in the face of the constantly predictable selfishness and total lack of consideration to which she found herself exposed. In recent months there had been too many nights when she'd been worn down until she found herself tagging along to whatever party or bar Cassie considered a decent hunting ground. Cassie would find two guys, be the life and soul of the foursome until Jen did something foolish like go to the bathroom. Then Cassie would seize her chance and on Jen's return, would make some lame excuse over her shoulder as she and her date headed out the door, dumping Jen with her opposite number – yet another embarrassed, discarded guy – and they would nurse the end of a pitcher comparing notes on surviving their friends.

On rare occasions it had led to a one-night stand or a weekend fling, but it was usually such a perfunctory consolation lay that she inevitably made her excuses and went home early to wait for a berating at the hands of a freshly-fucked Cassie.

Jen had had enough.

Cassie, meanwhile, was beginning to feel like the brakes on her life were broken and she was hurtling through traffic, but somehow always managing to swerve at the last minute.

What she wanted to be passionate and spontaneous somehow always became grubby and desperate.

She loved the chase; the flirtation always making

her feel in control. She was witty, eloquent and sharp. She was interesting and attractive and she knew it. She loved knowing how much they wanted her, loved making them wait; ordering more to drink or insisting on another dance, or playing them off someone else, just to test what she convinced herself was their commitment.

Having made it clear just how available she was, Cassie had never figured out a good way to avoid the inevitable ending to the evening.

Away from all the noise and lights, the light touches and smiles, Cassie would succumb to another night of being clumsily pawed by a near total stranger. Crappy apartment or faceless hotel room, it made no difference. Each time she wished for a lover who might prove exceptional, might make her feel something, but it was as if she was numb.

She had long reconciled herself to the idea that real women deserved to feel sexual, deserved to feel beautiful, deserved pleasure. She was a fraud. She was the idea of something, not the reality. She kept waiting to be found out, but the longer the game went on, the more she figured no-one was paying that much attention.

Deciding she was dead inside, she had come to think of the sex as the price to be paid for flirtation; a transaction she felt obliged to complete.

She came to feel nothing but contempt for them. They were with her for a bet. For a dare. Their friends were probably listening through the wall. She knew that while they laughed at her jokes, told her she was pretty, nodded and looked interested as they'd let her talk about herself most of the night – it had all just been what had to be done to get her into bed where she would shut up and take what was coming to her.

Cassie kept trying to convince herself, throughout and beyond all the empty sex, that it was her choice. She was a single, independent woman. She was using them. She would leave before they woke. She wanted nothing from them. But that didn't explain why she still gave them her number in that most futile of gestures. It didn't explain why she went home to scalding showers and crying herself to sleep. It didn't explain why she never told them how tiresome the sex was or asked for the things that would have made her happy.

Laying in hot baths on countless mornings after, Cassie would count her bruises, more often than not a set of five tiny purple patches showing just how roughly she had been grabbed, held and manhandled by some drunken idiot grateful for willing flesh to uncomplainingly accept whatever he had to offer.

But it wasn't them she hated. She wanted to, but she hated herself more.

The time soon came when Cassie's adventures no longer commanded the attention she thought they deserved. Having embarked on her Masters, Jen was rarely out her lab, determined to complete a Herculean experiment and analysis list that threatened to overwhelm her. It had been worrying her to the point of near total insomnia but help was at hand. The departmental secretary Gita secured a lab for her sole use but of course it came at a price, and that meant working most evenings, any weekends she liked and mornings so early they were practically the night before.

On the rare occasions she did make it to a bar or a club, the irony wasn't lost on Jen that she seemed to spend pretty much all her time with pond-life of one form or another.

Still, it meant she had a new-found friend and ally in the irrepressible Viennese secretary, and Jen's world became a more fun place to be. Many a weekend's work was interrupted by a gold-bedecked, scarlet-nailed hand clutching a bottle of gin appearing round the door. Gita didn't take no for an answer ('not from my husband, God himself or you, cookie') and Jen had given up trying, having quickly got wise to Gita's idea of what constituted a small drink.

At least one weekend in three, Gita's appearance would be heralded by the arthritic squealing of old wheels and much muttered cursing. Jen got used to her door being pushed open by a creaking lab trolley protesting under the weight of an ancient TV wobbling precariously atop an even older VHS player.

At the helm would be a grinning, panting Gita clutching her worn copy of *It's a Wonderful Life*. Jen had now seen the film more than a dozen times.

Gita's idea of a good time was two hours spent sobbing mightily and theatrically, blowing her nose on huge tissues, wailing about poor George Bailey and his lovely town gone to ruin.

Jen used to hurt from laughing.

One Sunday afternoon, pouring a fresh round of drinks for them both, it suddenly occurred to Jen that where George Bailey had his guardian angel Clarence, she had Gita. Except rather than rescuing the suicidal, this angel stopped Jen melting under her escalating workload, and sailed through the university corridors dressed in fuschia pink and tartrazine orange, frightening the unsuspecting with a laugh like a bomb going off.

Under the constant threat of corporate obligations, at the start of her second year Jen found herself an unwilling delegate at a major conference in the city.

She really didn't have the time or inclination to spend three days stuck in an anonymous hotel discussing local algae abnormalities with a succession of beardy lab-dwellers. Over the years Jen had amassed a fair body of evidence that as a sub-species, her male peers were inclined to get a bit over-excited at being out in public with actual women. She was sure it came from having spent too much of their time poking innocent anemones in the butt – it seemed to imbue in them all the social skills of sewage.

On one vicious pre-menstrual Friday afternoon, she'd grumbled her bloated, sore and spotty way through a tutorial, scaring her students into asking not one single question.

Bolting out the door, she'd thrown her weekend bag in the trunk and driven through the city in quite the most accomplished sulk even she could remember. Not even the fact that Gita had fooled the department into paying for a lake-view room for two nights (when technically Jen could have gone home) was doing anything to alleviate the mood.

'Fucking conference, fucking waste of my fucking time,' she growled, cutting up some tiny old Chinese lady in a neolithic Toyota and flooring it between sets of red lights which all seemed to have waited for her. Just as she pulled in to the hotel's parking bay out front, she realised she'd left her business cards sitting on the work-bench.

'Aarrgghh FUCK!' She wrenched the wheel round, nearly crippling the valet, and tore out past oncoming traffic, screeching to a seething halt at yet another red.

By the time she'd stormed through the corridors, banged the lab door open and grabbed the cards, tears were burning her eyes. She was just about ready to bite the next person who got in her way.

'This SUCKS,' she growled, and headed back to the hotel.

Sweaty, tired and fixating on a much-needed shower and mini-bar raid, she checked in at the supremely minimalist glowing mahogany reception. It had been entirely ruined by a bizarre single blue neon strip light. Jen wondered if that light came with a free pole and hooker shoes.

Interrupting her mental meander, the unrealistically enthusiastic young receptionist with perfect skin and perky breasts told her to have a nice day and, for one brief blissful moment, Jen pulled up an image of pushing a house-brick through her face.

'Whatever,' she mumbled, heading for an elevator.

The room was stunning; a work of simplistic art. The bed was an acre of fluffy white duvet and plump pillows, an oasis of inviting calm. The walls were white, the trim in scrubbed natural wood and there was quite simply no clutter. Most of the lighting was recessed — as was the wardrobe — there were no paintings on the wall but fresh flowers by the bed and on the simple writing desk. She watched as the boy moved quietly about the room, setting her luggage down and leaving her key on the desk. He silently rolled the pale wooden blinds fully open which bathed the room in the dipping sunlight reflected off the lake as it glittered in the early evening.

Jen stepped out onto the small balcony, the railing of which was covered with a twisting vine sprouting tiny yellow flowers. She suddenly felt very tired. Back in the room she slipped out of her shoes and let her feet sink into the thick, white carpet, then tipped the waiting boy and asked him to have a double gin and tonic sent up.

The mini-bar in the bedroom proved well stocked with Belgian fresh-cream truffles. When her drink arrived she took it and all the available chocolate back out onto the balcony, where she sank into the broad wicker armchair, put her feet up on the railing, wiggled her toes in amongst the papery yellow flowers and watched the sun slink off to its other day job.

The magical violet and aquamarine sky effortlessly soothed the day from her memory and as she drank she perused the dinner menu that had been in her conference welcome pack. Sponsored and hosted by some Swedish Environmental Agency, the options were firmly in favour of fish, fish and more fish. – Who the hell thinks an Environmental Biologist wants to eat fish? she wondered, but still, it did all seem to be accompanied by, marinated with or drowning in some sort of alcohol.

She threw back the rest of her drink and went to shower.

Not expecting to be socialising for long, she left her hair down and kept her make-up minimal. She pulled on a clean pair of jeans and her magic shirt (it had a one-button difference between Disapproving Tutor and Funky Girl Super Scientist), stepped into her favourite heels, grabbed her room key and went to face the world.

She was on a decent gin buzz when she stepped into the main conference room and, scanning the faces, nodded at the few she recognised from her own course as well as some of the agencies she dealt with on a regular basis. She began to make her way to the bar just as quickly as a room full of oblivious academics would allow ('a bumbling of scientists' her self-proclaimed hilarious Director of Studies would have said, but he'd also tried to name his children after varieties of river slug).

Just as she was contemplating the appropriate level of violence necessary to get to the bar, someone pinched her butt. She span round, her tingling hand

ready to do some damage. She was denied the opportunity, finding herself almost nose to nose with Gita
who was wobbling with fits of filthy giggles that
rattled her jewellery and threatened to dislodge her
wig.

'Gita!' Jen tried to admonish her, then thought
better of it. 'Ah what the hell – you're probably the
best offer I'm gonna get all weekend. Waste of a damn
fine hotel room if you ask me…'

Gita wagged a wrinkled finger in her face.

'I don't have a drink, terrible child. Get your
tushie in gear!'

Gita nodded towards the bar which could finally
just be seen in a small gap in the grubbing crowd.
Obediently, Jen pushed her way through, turning
back to Gita and mouthing '…the usual?' to which
Gita nodded enthusiastically and made a panting-like-
a-hot-puppy face.

In a few minutes Jen returned with two high-
balls filled to the brim. Gita took hers and went to
drink but as she did Jen said, 'I'd be careful – there's
half a bottle in there.'

Gita grinned. 'You take me for some sort of amateur,
I think.' She took a large swig followed by a moment
where nothing happened. Then her eyes widened and
out of her erupted a noise like a vacuum cleaner finding
an unexpected coin. Gita half-swallowed, half-inhaled

the mouthful, choking fitfully as it burnt the back of her nose. She spluttered. Jen sipped hers. 'Warned ya,' she said.

Gita, as it turned out, was working all evening, but she explained, with a huge wink, that one of her great skills was delegation and she'd left her secretary in charge, making it clear that she didn't want to be troubled with anything less important than the hotel burning down or Sean Connery checking in, bored and looking for some company. She had often said that if she ever found the actor she would seduce him with veal schnitzel ('until he is too heavy to run away and then I will ride him around and around like I am trying to win the Derby').

They made their way across the room, catching up on the week's gossip, but it wasn't long before Gita's pager made soft pinging noises and she excused herself leaving Jen feeling very conspicuous. She decided another drink was in order. At least going to the bar would make her look less abandoned. She stood there a few minutes later, sipping her fresh gin and stuffing a handful of cashews into her mouth. There had been more than she'd meant to take and it took a bit of tongue-wrestling to get enough purchase to start chewing them down. She felt like her kindergarten hamster with its face so full you thought its cheeks would split. Just then she heard a familiar booming voice behind her cry, 'Well if it isn't my favourite! Still drinking Jen'n'Tonic's, eh?'

She turned round, intending to show her Director of Studies, the irascible Dr Bannister, just how unable she was to answer back, given her mouthful of nuts.

When she saw what Henry was standing next to, she spluttered just enough to dislodge one slippy cashew which popped out her mouth and sat lodged between her breasts, peeking over the top of her bra. Time stopped. Jen swallowed the rest whole, washing the salty rubble down with a swig of gin. She choked, instantly, and tried to disguise it as a laugh but her streaming eyes, scorched nasal passages and ravaged throat didn't help much.

It took her a minute, but she recovered enough to realise that the tall, stunning vision before her was gentleman enough to be making a real effort to suppress a laugh and they could both see Henry staring at the errant nut. Without looking down, she picked it out and dropped it on the floor. She wondered what Gita would do in such excruciating circumstances, but realised she'd probably have invited the demi-god to get down on his knees and fish it out with his tongue. She blushed at the thought. The salt itched on her skin.

'Hi. Sorry to sneak up on you,' he said and on hearing the accent she realised he was with the sponsoring company and was simply doing a meet'n greet.

– What a stunning impression I've just made, she thought, and stuck her hand out, remembering as she did where it had just been. Too late.

'Jen Hollier. I majored in Environmental Biology at Toronto U but I'm doing my Masters at York, and I also do some contract work for the National Parks Environmental Advisory Board.'

– Oh sweet Jesus, she thought, I'm doing fluent Job Interview Speak.

'Markus Lindberg,' he said, 'but everyone calls me Mac. Tell me about the Advisory Board's work, it sounds interesting.'

Jen didn't have a polite answer to that, but she figured if it meant she got to look at him while she rattled through her usual spiel then who cared how bored he was? And so she launched into the same well-practised routine that covered dinner parties, funding pitches and all the other times when people felt obliged to ask why she'd decided to spend her life knee-deep in a stinking marsh.

Henry just stood grinning aimlessly and smiling encouragingly at Jen. She knew she'd never hear the end of the nut thing, but right now she didn't care. Mac, meanwhile, just wanted to keep her talking. He'd nearly volunteered to get the nut out for her but figured she'd either blush herself into an early grave or punch him. He wasn't entirely sure which.

Unbeknownst to Jen, he'd seen her through the window on one of Henry's amusingly random and infamously indiscreet tours of the university the day before. Henry had pointed through the window at her, saying, 'One of our best specimens. A girl, don't you know. Don't get many of those. She always makes me think of those fish, the little wiggly ones that seem to be listening to you. Can't think for the life of me what they're called. Nice fins, though, eh?'

Mac had stared at Henry and pretended to be horrified at the inappropriateness of the comment.

'What?'

'Those fish,' repeated Henry, winking, 'nice fins. Can't think what they're called. Extinct now, of course. Or will be by the time we get funding. Har har!'

Oblivious, Jen had carried on writing up her experiment results. Henry had offered to introduce Mac but he'd declined, claiming he didn't want to disturb her. In truth, he was jet-lagged and smelled of airplane and five hundred strangers and he found himself taken aback at how pretty she was. He'd put Henry off, saying, 'I'm sure we'll get a chance to meet at the conference,' praying that she would be there once he'd shaved and showered and didn't have skin the colour of an in-flight meal. Still, at least now he knew where to find her if she didn't show.

Jen got to the end of her spiel and caught Mac not really listening.

'Fascinating, huh?' she grinned up at him, and then he smiled, at which point Jen forgot which way was up. Maybe this stupid conference wasn't so awful after all.

'Yeah,' he grinned, 'you know, I think there's all kinds of things we should be doing together.' Jen didn't miss one second of the look that came with that and blushed again. 'Here's my card,' he said, passing one over and she reciprocated. He turned it over in his hands but didn't put it away.

'Would you excuse me?' he said to her, including Henry with a nod. 'I can only claim all the fun expenses if I mingle like I'm supposed to,' and with that he was gone.

Jen watched him go. Henry took a sip of his beer and said to her, 'Nice guy. Interesting. Some collaboration might be very good for the department.' Jen nodded agreement and sipped at her drink. 'Nice trick with the nut, too. What do you do for an encore?'

'Piss off, Henry.'

Henry winked and meandered away. A scarlet Jen strode off to the bathroom, desperate to get the itchy salt off her skin and to see if she'd yet evolved a muscle that with just a quick squeeze could give her a tan, lose six pounds, improve her skin, whiten her teeth and give her salon-glossy hair. She prepared for disappointment.

When she returned she scanned the room and found Mac, not that he could have easily hidden his tall, well-built frame, but there he was, chatting away. She expected to feel jealous if anyone else had his attention but in fact she relished the opportunity to watch him without being watched. Guessing him to be around six foot three, she thoroughly approved of the sandy blond hair and grey-blue eyes, healthy skin and wide smile. He'd had clean fingernails and quality shoes and she'd known from his hands and teeth that he didn't smoke. Her checklist was doing OK so far. Henry, sailing past, had answered a few questions from her – Mac was originally from some-where unpronounceable but now based in Stockholm, he was thirty-one and had been in the job four years. She assumed he was straight and desperately wanted to ask if he was single, but not since she'd started stumbling blindly through the dating minefield had she found a subtle way to ask.

She felt like a teenager again and wondered what to do. At eighteen she would have run for cover and hidden behind Cassie. Although she usually lost out in the end, like it or not Cassie was her pimp and it was easy to pretend that she resented it. Truth was, she grudgingly admitted to herself, she was eternally grateful that she'd pretty much always been spared all that coy, giggly, rude, forward nonsense that Cassie made look so effortless. But Cassie wasn't here. Which was a good thing. Except that Jen had always figured that by her mid-twenties she would be able to do this alone, but if it's one thing she dreaded it was the prospect of unarmed solo flirting.

She knew the evening was due to end with a jaunt out on the lake for cocktails on board a chartered yacht. Although Jen had loved the idea she'd not bothered signing up for it, horrified at the thought of being marooned with a bunch of dull academics and a limited bar. She wondered if Mac was going, because if he was she suddenly couldn't bear the thought of not joining him.

Making a beeline for the admin centre, her change of mind was hurriedly explained to Gita as the older woman peered over Jen's shoulder and took a good long look at Mac.

'Mama Gita can't think why you want to go, honey,' she rumbled, flashing a lascivious grin, making Jen blush furiously yet again. She felt she might melt if this went on.

'I know, I know – I'm behaving like an idiot adolescent and I'm so sure he has some stunning Viking wife and five perfect blonde kids in a bloody wood cabin somewhere and she bakes and is a brain surgeon and gives great head and is the perfect mother and has a gym-bunny butt, but hell, that kind of eye-candy just doesn't float out of sewer pipes every day.' Jen remembered to breathe. 'Also, I have to make up for our introduction.' Gita just raised an eyebrow. 'Ah god, Gita,' moaned Jen, 'I spat a nut into my bra.'

# Chapter Ten

This is what I deserve?

I deserve to be heart-broken? Alone? Abandoned? I deserve to be given the greatest gift only to have it snatched away?

Shauna was no sooner there than gone.

In our brief time together I'd had the strangest sensation that there was something wrong. Not between us – I was blissfully happy with the relationship – but I could sense…I don't know…it was as if our happiness was doomed. It was the strangest feeling, but I dismissed it as passing insecurity – those first few months in any new relationship are like that, you know? You become over-cautious. If you don't call for three days you start thinking that you've missed your chance, that somehow this person will have found out what you're really like and changed their mind. They will have realised what a terrible mistake they've made. I felt like that every time I went near her, that the first thing she'd say would be, 'We have to talk…'

There were so many days I wanted to surprise her at

work or home, but as I prepared to leave my own house I'd be crippled with paranoia that she would hate me for doing it, or that I'd see her with someone else, someone who deserved her more.

Now I know that it was just the universe mocking me. It said, 'You don't deserve this nice thing and I'm going to let you have it long enough only to appreciate what you will lose.'

I heard it. I felt it.

If I'd ever felt that I was unworthy, I had it proven to me beyond any doubt when I lost my soul-mate.

A random act. A brutal murder. An animal never caught.

I was devastated. I just wanted to die. Every breath was an effort. At first I couldn't move or find the will to eat or wash or dress myself. I'd go for four, sometimes five nights without sleep.

I kept the curtains closed, barely moving from whatever room I'd lain down in. On the rare occasions I could summon any energy, any motivation, it seemed to be driven by a force inside me – it was like I could feel it bullying me – it wouldn't let me rest. I cried. I screamed for her to come back to me. I made promises to a God I don't believe in, if only He would send her back to me. But she didn't come back. How could life be so unfair? I'd been abandoned. How could she do this to me?

Whenever it all got too much, the solution was

simply to smash my face off a wall until I blacked out. I got used to waking with my forehead bruised and speckled with dried blood. Those were the days I felt calm and quiet in myself.

This wasn't the first time I'd found physical pain to be the way to engage my sluggish mind. I'd start by picking away at soft tissue, generating a contusion by constantly rubbing, scratching and irritating a patch of flesh. Best place was on the soles of my feet. I'd take a small pair of silver scissors and pick away at the sensitive, reddened, swollen spot until I'd made a tiny, livid hole From there it was easy to tear minute strips of skin away from around the edges until the wound bled and stung. I loved to walk barefoot around the apartment like that, thriving on the sudden jolts of pain from pressure, splinters or uneven floors. I felt nourished by the pain. You would only understand this if you'd been through exactly what I went through. My agony was unique.

While there was reassurance and focus to be found in the simple processes of physical injury, I seemed to heal depressingly quickly. A problem easily remedied. Sewing needles, house keys and corkscrews made excellent picks for loosening scabs and inflaming raw wounds. I found I could get through a good day without one single coherent thought about my grief, simply by riding the waves of pain. I came to realise that I was in danger of wasting my suffering. What I needed was a witness to validate me.

I didn't enjoy getting ready to leave my apartment. I hadn't seen or touched the outside world for nearly two weeks. I found clean clothes, but didn't feel like washing before I pulled them on. The pale fabric of all my socks was discoloured by the patches of blood and sticky fungal moisture soaked into the fibres. The pain of dozens of open wounds, suppurating sores and ragged skin made shoes an agony I could not have anticipated. I was almost delusional with the excruciating pleasure of it.

When I could finally stand, I stared at my reflection in the bathroom mirror. My eyes were bloodshot, the bags beneath them dark and heavy against my pallid skin My beard was ragged; my hair greasy and lank. As I left, I knew nobody seeing me would be in any doubt that this was a soul in torment, a man broken by suffering.

I drove across town, wincing with each sweetly torturous exertion on the pedal, until I finally found the office, chosen from a particularly cloying commercial on late-night TV. The softly-spoken receptionist didn't flinch at the way I smelled but instead showed me directly into a room with white walls; the desk and fittings a dark, worn wood. On one wall hung four faded framed certificates. I shook hands with the middle-aged man across the desk and slumped into the sagging leather chair before him. The whole space felt disconnected, as if it wasn't really real. I couldn't even hear any traffic noise from outside. I stared at Dr Howarth and waited to be fixed.

I approved of the way he introduced himself properly even though his nameplate was right there in front of me. Then he asked how I was doing.

'How do you think I'm doing?' I spat at him.

He didn't react. Instead he spoke slowly and evenly, saying calming words in a tone that promised professional, steady progress.

He was talking but I was distracted by a familiar knot in my gut and the taste of bile in the back of my throat.

I tuned back in to hear, 'The first stage is often one of shock and denial. It's common to feel a total sense of isolation and an anger that can be very confusing and upsetting. It's important to try and remember that these are just the early phases of the road to recovery. There are several stages you can expect to pass through and although some of it will be painful and difficult, each of these stages is part of a process. I will be here to help you along this journey and in time there will be acceptance. Your life will go on.'

I stared down at my hands, incensed. He was talking to me like I was some idiot adolescent pining for a first love! This shabby little fucker was reading chapter one to me as if I was just like everyone else. I had clearly made a bad choice. I felt spasms fire through me, demanding I leap to my burning feet and leave this place. I pushed myself upright, my legs shaky as my wounded feet took my weight. I leaned forward, resting both my hands on the edge of his desk, pushing his nameplate askew.

'Do you have any idea what I've been through? What I'm going through? My life is….it's over. There's nothing left. She was everything to me, do you get that? DO YOU GET THAT? How can I live without her? Do you even know what this feels like, or did you just read some books and figure being a shoulder to cry on was an easy buck?'

'We all experience loss, Mr….' Howarth looked down at his notes. I realised with a jolt I had no idea what name I'd given when I made the appointment. I ignored the prompt.

'What? You seriously think my loss is no different to anyone else's? Were you just gonna read me the instructions and wait for me to join the program? I am not like everyone else. I'm different. This is different. This is…bigger. This is…' I really struggled for the right word I was so mad. 'Special. It's special. And if you don't get that, then this is a waste of my fucking time.'

I sank back into my seat, struggling to get my breathing back under control and desperate for the throbbing ache in my feet to subside, my legs shaking with the jolts of pain shooting through my calves.

I stared past Dr Howarth out the window to the park beyond, suddenly remembering one time in my teens when I spent an entire Sunday slumped under a tree on the first warm weekend of Spring. It felt then like the world was full of couples.

I hated and envied them in equal measure. Arms flung around each other, kissing as they walked, some eating ice-cream or carrying balloons or flowers. It was sickening. But I wanted it so badly it made me choke.

As the sun had gone down and the bugs got worse, I'd gone to visit my grandmother and we watched TV shows together, only with her it was always the ones where they told you stories about childhood sweethearts who got married early and had tons of kids and then got tons of grandkids and great grandkids. Those people always looked young – for old people – and they were still totally in love with each other. Truth be told, I loved all that stuff. Ever since I was old enough to think about it, I'd wanted to love someone that much. But more than that, I wanted them to love me that much right back.

It wasn't just that I wanted to be happy, it was more than that – I wanted it so badly, so much more than anyone else that I finally realised that maybe I was going to have to wait just that little bit longer because I deserved a big love; something special.

But now my special love, as quickly as she had come into my life, she was gone. Torn apart by a maniac. Shredded. Obliterated.

In the aftermath of that, everything I did, I did

without her. I breathed without her. I ate, cried and hurt myself without her  Every time I opened my eyes, there was just a space where she should be. I could feel it, like her absence moved with me, sharing what my existence had become. The more I talked to her, pleaded with her, begged her to come back to me, the more I realised how alone I truly was and it wasn't long before her passivity made me furious, as if even her spirit was abandoning me. She had ruined everything.

Focusing, I looked back at Howarth. He acknowledged me, briefly, then went back to making a note on the pad on his desk. While he was doing that I got up and left. I heard him call out to me as I closed the door behind me.

I ignored the receptionist as she tried to say something to me, mostly because I knew if I so much as opened my mouth, everything in me would come screaming out. I had to keep control. But I felt completely belittled. This idiot Howarth had insulted not just me but the memory of my beloved Shauna. How dare he think my grief so… so ordinary.

My special girl. Gone. And what the fuck can a sweating idiot with a degree in head-shrinking tell me about how to live now? I'm ALONE! She's abandoned me, left me on my own. This is not what I planned. I don't deserve this. This is not how things will be.

Denial? I'll give him fucking denial.

# Chapter Eleven

The gentle strains of Massive Attack slunk out the stereo. Candles spluttered from every flat surface in the room and the girls lay amongst the debris of a dip frenzy.

'Jesus, Jen, my love life is turning into one big ugly power ballad. It won't be one of the good ones either. You know, not one you can dance to. It'll be someone like Cinderella or Poison or Twisted Sister. It'll be that duff track on a compilation that makes you shatter your ankles stumbling across the room to skip the CD on to whatever the hell is next. It'll be one of those tracks that makes you think Meat Loaf really wasn't so bad after all. Worse, it'll be one of those ones that accidentally makes you cry when it catches you unawares and the shame of it'll nearly bend you in half. All cock-rock and big hair.'

Jen choked on her wine and hiccupped through her laughter.

'I mean,' Cassie was in full rant, 'I've had a third of my allotted time on the planet, assuming I make it past the finishing line. So the first third I've been useless, it's a safe bet the last third I'll be equally useless with added drooling and huge underwear, so this bit in the middle…isn't this where it's all supposed to happen? I mean, I only have one small heart and it's already got footprints all over it, as well as some major patchwork and it's mostly held together by bits of string.'

Having seen Cassie in this mood often enough, Jen let her go on.

Cassie stared balefully out the window. 'Ah crap, it's a full moon. I must be tidal. That would at least explain why the miserable, self-indulgent bits of my grey matter are sloshing back and forth in messy puddles.' She paused then continued, 'Come on, this is your cue to tell me that somewhere there's a perfect man for me, that it'll all be OK, that I'm not gonna end up some mad old spinster, reeking of soup and found dead on the kitchen floor at eighty half eaten by the nineteen cats I've adopted.'

Without waiting for an answer, Cassie levered herself to her feet and lurched off to the kitchen, returning with the bottle of red. She refilled her glass, slugged some of it back then passed the bottle over before slumping down into her armchair again.

'Just look at the last one,' she growled, 'so yeah, he drew cartoons that made me laugh, but he also broke into my apartment building and left poisonous plants on my doorstep as a sign of affection! And this is the same guy who wrote a sixteen-verse poem about me, burned the edges of it, rolled it up as a scroll and jammed it in a bottle that had my name dripped up the side in wax.' She paused. 'At least, I'm assuming it was wax…'

Jen giggled. 'See, I remember when you just met him,' she paused, reaching over to grab a handful of tortilla chips, 'and you told me he was so funny… I remember. You did. You liked him. You thought he was cute. You said he was different from all the others. You said he was nice. That's why you banged him on the kitchen floor, remember? Cos he was nice. Or was it because he had a pulse? I forget.'

Cassie glared at Jen over the rim of her glass and drew breath to defend herself, but Jen interrupted.

'I think you're sulking cos this one left you first and that's all there is to it.' Red wine always made Jen feel brave, usually right up to the point where Cassie poked her into submission or threw something at her. 'You're a control freak, Cassie. And a tart.'

Cassie threw everything within reach, which amounted to two corks, a cushion and half the day's newspaper. It all missed.

Jen just smiled at her. 'So is this a good time to tell you I met someone?' she asked.

'Someone with a capital S?'

Jen nodded. 'I think so. Or I'm prepared to drink myself into an early grave if I'm wrong.'

Rant, insults and self-pity instantly forgotten, Cassie took the bottle, leaned over and filled Jen's glass then topped her own up again and demanded to be told everything.

'Promise you won't interrupt?'

'No.'

'OK, so the short version just to keep your weeny attention span active, is that I went to a conference, met a rep – a tall, blond, beautiful, sexy, Swedish rep, and had a very nice weekend and…'

'Hurrah!' shouted Cassie, starfishing to her feet and haphazardly saluting Jen with glass raised. 'You did it. I'm so proud of you. Hurrah for one-night stands,' and with that she slid to the floor, via the edge of her chair.

Jen was more than a little put out at Cassie's assumption that Mac was a phase she was going through, but just thinking about him made it easier not to care.

'It's probably not a one-night stand,' she said huffily, 'because he's asked to be transferred here and should be moving over some time in the next couple months once all the paperwork's sorted.'

Cassie stared at her. 'Isn't that all a bit sudden?'

'Yeah,' grinned Jen, 'and fantastic.'

'Well good for you. Seriously Jen, it's great. I can't wait to meet him.'

After Jen left, Cassie opened the third bottle and sat glugging wine, hunched into one end of the sofa, furious.

She had always expected to be delighted for Jen when she fell in love but given the catalogue of disaster that her own love-life constituted, she was livid.

It was typical of Jen to do this to her. Jen who studied and got good grades. Jen who ate well and had good skin. Jen who never got wasted or had casual sex or any fucking fun, now sailed off to some dumb conference and met the perfect man, seemingly without any grief. It just wasn't fair.

'Why should I have to have all the shit?' she fumed aloud.

What started as drunken envy festered over the coming months into barely-disguised jealousy which spilled over on bad days, making her bitter and resentful to the one person in the world she said she loved.

'Emergency Room. Be my pumpkin? Bring Prince Charming.'

An obscure message from Cassie wasn't unusual. Jen looked longingly at her street as the cab did a three-pointer and took her back across the city to the hospital. A half hour later, she stepped through the sliding doors into the super-chilled air of the hospital lobby, squinting under the fluorescent glare. She should be in bed.

The Emergency Room was never a good place to be but somehow Saturday nights painted it as a lost vision of hell. She found herself staring at five frat boys, reeking of beer and coated in blood. A young nurse stopped and followed her gaze, finally laughing.

'I know it looks bad, but it's mostly salsa. Can I help you?'

Jen followed her directions to Curtain Three and there found her best friend reclining on a gurney, one huge swollen foot resting on an ice-pack atop a folded pillow. Cassie's skin was the colour of weak Chardonnay and she was grinning in a way that Jen found strangely worrying.

'I'd have worn a better bra if I'd known I'd be sitting here without my shirt on. Is it really necessary? I haven't had a headache in my tummy since I was four. I'm cold. My head hurts. I want to go home. Where did that guy go? The cute one? I forget his name. But he was cute, don'cha think? Are you cold? I'm cold. Do you like this bra?'

'What happened? Why are you here? More importantly, why am I here? I have a life, Cassie. I shouldn't have to be at your beck and call like this.' Jen realised, hearing the whiny tone of her own voice that she was right, she didn't have to be here, but it hadn't even occurred to her to leave Cassie alone to sort out whatever this weekend's mess was. A familiar resentment flooded through her, but she was way too tired to do anything about it.

Cassie's tone became petulant. 'It's not really how I planned on this evening ending, you know. The only person who's even spoken to me was some livid, underpaid nurse who,' (she raised her voice, mortifying Jen) 'has an acid scowl and spikes where her damn heart should be! I need more than an ice-pack and these fucking horse tranquilizers,' (she dropped her voice) 'but apparently everyone but me is deemed deserving of sympathy.' She sank back into her pillows, grimacing as the movement went through her. 'I had something a bit funkier in mind,' she pouted.

Jen had just nodded, wishing she was in her own bed, getting a good run up at her own hangover, but Cassie wasn't done, drawing in and releasing a long, theatrical sigh as she went for the sympathy vote.

'I've had it, Jen, I've really had it. Maybe gran's right; maybe I'll be Calamity-Cassie forever. Or maybe this is the minor demons' idea of comedy. What passes for my joke of a love-life is always the wrong man who looked at me the right way at the wrong end of the bottle. So the demons push me into a mirror when I meet something cute in a nice, normal way.'

Jen shot Cassie a look that would have eaten through steel.

'You were pushed? Cassie, that club has had a mirror there since it opened. We've been there a thousand times! Lemme guess…you saw someone you thought you recognised, got mad cos you thought she was staring at you, so you went storming over only to smack into your own reflection, right?'

'Where is he?'

'Huh?'

'Prince Charming. I said to bring Prince Charming!'

'He said to tell you he's married.'

'Happily?'

'Yes! Not that that would stop you, I guess.'

At this, Cassie went quiet, folded her arms and turned her head away.

Jen slumped down onto a tiny vinyl stool the colour of rancid olives and rested her head on the starched bed cover.

'Hello Jen, how are you? Thanks for coming, I really appreciate it.' Getting no response she looked up. 'I'm so tired. And drunk. And I should be in bed. Why am I here?'

Cassie inhaled, but no explanation followed. Her eyes were dark and on meeting Jen's gaze she looked away again, still apart from her hands twisting the edge of the sheet.

'I'm in pain.'

'I can see that, honey. Sordid story now, please, so I can go to bed.'

Cassie sniffed loudly. 'Some drunk guy went crazy and whacked me in the face.' She turned her head and Jen saw clearly just how badly bloodshot and bruised her left eye was. She winced.

'He just went crazy? Was he on something?'

'I don't know,' said Cassie in her favourite, pity-me soft voice. 'He just totally came at me with no warning and the next thing I know I'm on the floor and he's getting ready to hit me again when security appeared and tried to hold him down, but he got away and came after me with a steak knife. I ran so fast down the stairs, I fell and did this. She held up her left hand, turning it over to show Jen where it had been ground against the wall. Dozens of tiny peaks of skin were raised over her fingers, hand and wrist, all spotted with dried blood. Her flesh looked grated.

Jen swallowed hard. 'Were you drunk?'

'Of course I was drunk. It's Saturday night.' Cassie closed her eyes for a moment, letting her mangled hand slide from Jen's view.

'Babe that must have been so frightening. I'm so glad you're mostly OK. Have you talked to the cops? Do you have any idea who he was?'

She didn't get an answer as they were interrupted by a nurse's face appearing around the curtain. Cassie took one look and sat bolt upright, brushing her hair back with her good hand.

'Hey there princess. How those meds working out for you?'

Cassie just grinned at him. He laughed.

'OK, got a better question for you…does this hurt?'

He lifted Cassie's foot, gently twisting it to either side. Jen squirmed but Cassie just kept on grinning.

'No more happy pills for you tonight. Let me get the paperwork done and you can go home, Cinderella.' He winked and left them alone.

'I'm guessing you lost a shoe. Have you reported this yet? I mean, he might do this to someone else, Cassie, you have to report this.'

'He won't do this to anyone else, it's OK. Could you get me some coffee? I'm super-tired.'

Jen went but was halfway down the corridor when she realised something. She went straight back, empty-handed.

'How do you know he won't do this to anyone else? Tell me the truth Cassie.'

Cassie looked up, her eyes dark and suddenly closer to tears than Jen could ever remember.

'I think I did a bad thing.'

Jen raised her eyebrows and sat down, watching as Cassie's face relaxed, the effort at appearing sorry as exhausting as ever. Cassie grinned, shrugged and admitted, 'OK, so I know I did a bad thing.'

With a grunt, she pushed herself up against the pillows, smoothed the sheets, inspected her nails, clasped her hands and still managed to pause a little longer for full dramatic effect. Jen got to seventy-four in her slow count to derail thoughts of smothering Cassie with a spare pillow.

'I knew him, the crazy guy. I was trying to end things and he took it pretty badly.'

Jen shook her head. 'I lose track of these guys, Cassie. Is it worth me asking what his name was?' Without waiting for a reply, she stood. 'I still need coffee. You want something?'

Cassie shook her head, looking oddly close to tears. Jen could feel herself getting angrier, so went in search of something to give her the strength to get through yet another of Cassie's crises, promising herself for the millionth time that this time would be the last.

When she came back, there was a pair of crutches propped against Cassie's bed, and a prescription resting on the little tray table.

Waiting till Jen had settled down with her coffee, Cassie poured herself some water, screwing her face up as she tasted it.

'This stuff is warm.'

'Uh–huh.'

Silence settled between them.

'I feel horrible.'

'Take some more painkillers.'

'No, I mean properly horrible. Like maybe I did something seriously wrong.'

'Cassie, can I skip to the end here? You were not in love, you are not heartbroken, it will be the same story with a different guy next week and you know it. You are always having flings. Or encounters. Or adventures. Or whatever the hell you need to call it to salve your delusional conscience. What's the big deal this time?'

Cassie just stared at her, saying nothing. Jen laughed weakly, holding her hands up in mock surrender. 'Come on, Cassie. How bad can it be?'

'This guy…OK, so technically he wasn't mine to play with but I kinda liked him, you know?'

Jen knew, and the words were out her mouth before she could stop them. 'Are you pregnant?'

Cassie shook her head.

Jen nodded and quietly said, 'If he's not yours,

then whatever is going on is just wrong, you know that, right? It has to stop. How many times do I have to tell you that?' Jen stared down at her hands and waited a moment. 'You've never, ever felt bad about taking just what you wanted before now, Cassie. Why is this any different?' In the ensuing silence she had a horrible thought. 'Oh, Cassie, is it someone I know?'

Cassie sat with silent tears running down her face. She looked Jen in the eye and said, 'It wasn't Mac, if that helps any.' Then she couldn't meet her gaze any more.

Jen was livid. 'Like that makes it any fucking better? How the hell can you ever do this to another woman, Cassie?'

'It's easier than you will ever know. Anyway, this has been going on for a couple of months, and all this time he keeps telling me how much he loves me, how special I am, how I'm so different to all the other women, how he can't live without me. It was so nice to hear it all the time.'

'So? '

Cassie looked at her, her eyes dark and threatening more tears.

'So...just to shut him up last week, I kinda told him to prove it.'

It began to dawn on Jen just what Cassie might

have done. She took a deep breath.

'Cassie, I'm tired, drunk and sick to death of spending endless nights and mornings-after listening to your self-indulgent whining about men. This isn't a game.'

'I know.' Cassie seemed almost contrite. 'I know that now. Except now it's kinda too late. I told him to prove it...well, dared him really. I honestly never thought he'd do it! I've played this game with so many guys and they all know the rules. I just love the thought that they might, you know? Just the idea that they might abandon everything for me. I love the idea of it. It's so...passionate. So impulsive and romantic. At least, I thought it would be.'

'He actually left his wife for you?'

Cassie was suddenly indignant. 'Don't sound so damn surprised! Anyway, wife and three kids, if you wanna be picky about it. Confessed everything and turned up on my doorstep with two suitcases. You should have seen him...he was so excited...just like a little kid. Right then, so was I. It was such a high. But man, that wore off so damn quick and I just had to get him away from my apartment. We went out for dinner. That went OK but after a couple of beers he got kinda intense. So I told him I didn't really want to get serious with anyone right now, and that's when he freaked out. Started threatening me, kept screaming at me. Then he totally flipped and smacked me in the face and threatened me and came after me with a knife, so now I'm scared to go home cos he might be there and he's so mad at me. Can I come stay at yours for a while?'

In the burned silence, Jen silently zipped her jacket, picked her bag up from the end of the bed and said, 'How can you think this is OK?'

'I never thought he'd really do it! And where are you going? I'm not ready – I need five minutes. I wanna try to get that cute nurse's number. Hand me my jacket, will ya?'

Jen sat back down. 'Do you even understand what you've done? The damage you've caused? All that pain, and heartbreak and disruption…if you didn't really want him, how could you take such a stupid risk?'

Cassie cocked her head to one side and gave the matter a second's thought.

'I guess I just wanted to know for my own personal satisfaction.'

Jen was incensed. 'You ruined someone's marriage because your pathetic ego was craving a little extra attention? Fuck you, Cassie. You only ever tell me all this crap because you know I'll be mad at you and that's about as much retribution as you're prepared to take. Well, I'm not his wife and I will not make you feel better by indulging your feeble attempt at a confession. Do you even have the faintest idea how insulting this is? I so don't want to be around you right now. You've behaved like a total slut.'

As Jen turned to leave, Cassie came back at her with a voice low and mean.

'No, wait, I know…why don't I be just like you, Jen? I'll be a good girl and stay home and study hard and everyone will approve of me. Wouldn't that be nice? If only I'd been smart enough to do things your way, Jen, I would never have had to take a risk or have an adventure or face the world on my damn own because I'd have wasted half my life hiding behind my friends like only a truly sanctimonious coward does. You were always perfectly fucking happy for me to play the party girl if it helped get you laid.'

With angry tears stinging her eyes, Jen pushed the flimsy curtain aside and walked away.

The last indignity of Cassie's night was to have to ask Kath to come pick her up. In the car on the way home, Cassie confessed to the fight, if not the details, somehow managing to make it sound like Jen had been mean to her and in some selfish fit had abandoned her, leaving her helpless and nearly stranded.

Kath wasn't fooled. 'Well I think if you guys had a fight then you should go apologise to her.'

'What for? She knows me well enough by now.

I am so not saying sorry. I have my pride, mom.'

'Yeah, honey. You're as proud as a mule.'

# Chapter Twelve

I went to Illinois. I was just supposed to be passing through, but something about the place made me stay, stick around for a week or so, see what was going on.

That's when I saw her. Just out for a drive around the city and there she was, waiting to cross the street. She was squinting into the sun, only shielding her eyes to check if the lights had changed and she could walk. As I watched, she looked down, then fished around in her shoulder bag until she found her phone. After pressing a couple of buttons she smiled at whatever the message contained. It was a good smile. I know no-one would seriously expect to see their ideal woman just like that, but there she was and suddenly it was all so simple.

I pulled the car into a parking space and laughed right out loud. Jeez, I just could not believe such a simple solution had evaded me for so long. All this time I'd been going about everything the wrong way. All that grieving, sulking and pining. That wasn't going to fix anything, was it? It just wasn't productive. All that wallowing in self-pity, wishing the universe had been kinder to me. What an idiot. Bad things will happen and I saw clearly for the first time in months that I couldn't judge my life by what bad things happened to me, but I could by how I chose to deal with it. Once I had that figured, it was all so easy! How could I have missed something so obvious?

I pulled down the vanity mirror, combed my hair a little, rubbed my coffee-stained teeth with a clean finger and smiled at myself, addressing my reflection.

'Now do you get it, idiot?' I grinned. 'All you've gotta do is find the right woman and you can go right back to the way things were.'

I could just pick up from where Shauna and I left off. It'd be perfect. It'd be like nothing ever happened.

I grabbed the city map from the passenger seat and went to talk to the perfect woman. It didn't take me more than a couple of minutes to catch up to her, which is when I smiled her my best smile and held out the map. I told her I was new in town, that I was lost, asked her to show me just where the hell I was. She laughed, sympathised. She asked me my name. I liked that she was friendly. So open. Her name was Emily. A little young, but I could forgive that because she looked and sounded just right. All my fantasies made flesh.

She let me buy her a coffee. A couple of days later I took her to a movie. For her that seemed to mean we were dating. She wasn't the smartest. Still, I had so much to tell her, like her favourite stores and favourite meals and favourite songs. It was all going to be so perfect.

At least, it would have been if she'd let me. I don't really know why she couldn't be just as I needed her to be. It was like trying to walk to a nice spot you can see in the park, only once you start out there's people and paths and trees and ponds and hills in the way that you didn't see before. You still really want to get there but the more stuff there is in the way the angrier you get until that nice spot just seems like one giant pain in the ass.

You see what I'm getting at?

I could have made it perfect – for both of us – but she wouldn't let me. She kept letting stupid little things get in the way, and I kept trying to clear our path but it wasn't as easy as it should have been.

Shauna was gone. I'd been through enough. Just imagine what it must feel like to have your soul-mate brutally destroyed...well, that would break anyone, wouldn't it? You have no idea what I've been through, but trust me, it's not something you ever recover from. Bad enough to lose someone you love to natural causes at the end of a full life like I'd always hoped – like one of those cute TV stories – sure that's devastating. But to lose someone so abruptly...so cruelly...you don't ever come back from something like that.

I couldn't. I didn't. I deserved better.

It takes a lot of pressure to close off a trachea completely – three times more than it takes just to render someone unconscious – and it has to be sustained for longer than you'd think. The planning and effort it all took was so much more than she deserved by then. Although I was already itching to move on, I couldn't drag myself away before the funeral.

I was real sorry when things with Emily didn't quite work out, but I like to think we parted friends.


Steve Bassing had given up work not long after Emily died. It was her funeral that did it. He'd wanted to apologise to her parents but as the first handful of soil landed on her coffin, he lost his nerve.

Ever since, he has had to inhale deeply and exhale completely before chewing and swallowing something. He feels sick every time someone coughs or clears their throat. He watched her die and is still afraid to go to sleep as he is plagued by nightmares where he relives the scene over and over, hearing every bubbling gasp, feeling her claw at his legs, never for one second able to tear his gaze from hers. He wakes in the early hours, crying and unable to breathe properly, heaving and choking as he tries to quell the panic that grips his lungs. Alone in the dark, he feels certain his punishment for failing her will be to die the same way.

# PART TWO

# Chapter Thirteen

Winter started early with November bringing thick grey skies and forty-watt yellow light. The city, like its inhabitants, seemed to gear itself up to freeze, to spend four months with cold bones and chilled blood. December obliged with freak blizzards falling from dawn to dusk from a corpse-coloured sky.

Jen and Mac had rented an apartment downtown and in the throes of a new relationship still found everything cute, even having to live out of dozens of boxes that turned what had seemed a decent-sized space into an obstacle course littered with sharp corners and jagged staples. They had both sworn to have the place clear for a pre-Christmas party but with four days to go it seemed unlikely.

That evening Mac took a call on his cell that Jen only heard bits of as he wandered through the apartment, crashing into things as he found himself in yet another dead-end in the maze of their boxed lives. A full ten minutes later he threw the living room door open and stood grinning at her.

'That was my buddy, Paul. Man, I haven't seen him in years! He says his flight's been cancelled,' he waved an explanatory hand at the foul weather obscuring their view, 'and the poor guy was offered some really crappy hotel till they could get him on another flight, but I said not to be ridiculous, that he should come stay with us for the holidays. You don't mind, do you babe?'

As they both found out later that evening, Paul's karma had come in the form of a loopy Viennese widow. Paul told Jen he knew Mac was frequently in Toronto, so might know somewhere cool to stay other than the soulless airport nightmare he'd been offered. Firstly from Mac's old PA in Stockholm, and then from Gita and her self confessed confidentiality issues, Paul had heard all the gossip about his friend's love life, career move and prospects. He also had his address, home and cell numbers and a story about an incident in the bathrooms of a boat that reassured him that Mac hadn't changed much.

He and Mac were clearly delighted to see each other again and any borderline resentment Jen might have felt at having to share their first Christmas together soon dissipated. Paul was sweet and funny and had turned up with a huge box of dark, chocolate-coated macadamia nuts. He was welcome anytime.

As she finished up some work, the boys got stuck

into their beer supplies and rattled through enough abbreviated anecdotes to fill each other in on the gaps of the last two years.

The first evening set the tone for the rest of the holiday season as they lounged around the apartment, stuffing their faces, getting drunk and Paul regaling Jen with carefully edited tales of Mac's terrible exploits on the road. Mac seemed blissfully happy to listen and nod along, and Jen was finally delighted to have someone who knew Mac willingly tell her some of the things he was unlikely to ever volunteer.

At one story, mulled wine shot down Jen's nose and spilt onto her jeans as laughter bubbled up and spilled over.

'You did what?!'

'Thanks, Paul,' Mac said, raising one eyebrow at Jen.

She laughed, having recovered enough to control her nose.

'You threw a woman…'

'…in the trash, yes,' he finished for her.

'I hate to ask the obvious question, but…why?!'

'We met her in a bar,' he started, 'and I took her home.'

Jen nodded, pretending that she was fine with the idea that Mac had been with other women but she did a lousy job of convincing anyone, especially herself.

'So we were getting it on,' he continued, 'but she was bugging the hell out of me. She wanted me to pretend to be a cop or something and arrest her.' Paul sniggered, nudging Jen gently in the ribs as Mac went on. 'She was kinda crazy, so I carried her down to the hotel basement and threw her in the trash.'

Jen needed more information.

'Which way up? Was the trash empty? God, Mac, just how annoying was she?'

'Ah, OK,' he said, 'I threw her in feet first. Into an empty bin, I swear. It wasn't very deep.'

'And how annoying was she?'

'Well, I threw her in the trash – what do you reckon?'

The story unfolded, both boys taking turns to fill in the gaps. Woman disposed of, Mac had gone up to Paul's room in the hotel where they'd watched Grand Prix qualifiers on TV and in the course of about an hour, he'd received in excess of thirty text messages and phone calls from the girl in the bin.

He had eventually gone down and got her out. She was a bit cross, by all accounts.

'The punchline,' said Paul, laughing, 'is that the next day in the middle of our investor meeting, his cell phone vibrates as he gets a text from her, saying "When can I see you again?"' Jen looked at Mac who just shrugged and carried on rubbing her feet.

'Just watch out, missy,' he grinned, 'or you might end up in the trash…'

Jen punched his shoulder hard. 'Not if I throw you in there first.'

For a couple of days they mooched, sang rude versions of carols, slept late, watched old movies and had what looked pretty much like a perfect Christmas.

Jen had decided she liked Paul very much and was wondering just what would happen when he finally met Cassie. As Paul sat listening to them discussing her one evening, he was thinking she sounded mad, bad and dangerous to know, although that wasn't necessarily a bad thing. When he said as much, Mac winked broadly at him, saying, 'She's the best kind of trouble, if your shining armour is up to the job.' Jen had bitten her tongue, wondering if she was expected, yet again, to say nothing while Cassie over-indulged, like a gourmand at a buffet, helping herself to handfuls of everything in sight, just because she could?

The day before the party, they finally decided to do something about the boxes and so spent hours stacking them floor-to-ceiling in every corner, all the while picking at leftovers each time they passed the kitchen. That evening, exhausted and collapsed on the sofa, the boys channel-surfed as Jen took her turn to make dinner which, this close to Christmas, meant being in the kitchen, slaving over a hot phone, dialling out for three huge pizzas, everything on them.

She came back through and perched on the back of the sofa, cracked open a beer and addressed the two men sprawled below her.

'So come on then, how did you two meet?' She instantly felt a flicker of jealousy as both men stared wide-eyed at each other, clearly trying to pass the buck on who would tell a version of the truth that wouldn't get Mac into nine kinds of trouble. Paul grabbed the remote and silenced the TV.

'I went to Sweden,' he started, 'for work...' but he was interrupted by Mac's roared laughter as he sat bolt upright.

'You came to Sweden because there was a conference at a Spa retreat and you, my fine friend, had got all your sauna education from watching too much cheesy '70s porn!'

'It's true,' said Paul, blushing furiously.

Mac told the story. 'Part of the package was a presentation in the corporate facility of a fantastic Japanese-style Spa and an overnight stay for delegates, Paul included. I was supposed to be looking after all the guests but I found him at the bar late in the afternoon contemplating a list of herbal infusions and anyone could see the man wanted a real drink. Happily, I never travel unprepared so we retired to my room for the day and got spectacularly blitzed. Client crises came and went, judging by how often my phone rang, but they seemed to get less important as the day wore on and the bottles got emptied. By the evening, I was teaching him made-up Viking songs and offering ludicrous transalations and he kept crying at the sad ones.'

Mac roared with laughter, Paul blushed even harder, shaking his head at the memory.

Drunkenly enthused by the idea of late night fishing, they'd ricocheted through the surrounding forest into a wide clearing where they'd 'borowed' a handy rowboat and made it into the centre of the lake in one piece.

Apparently the adventure quickly deteriorated into more copious drinking and leaning over the edge of the boat and asking the fish politely if they wouldn't mind flinging themselves on board.

Skinny-dipping at sunrise (though not alone as their singing had attracted some company from the resort) had set everyone up to take yet more bottles of unmarked, home-brewed, possibly illegal, definitely lethal spirits into a nearby sauna. Apparently Paul's adolescent fantasies came to nothing but by all accounts the day got more interesting as it progressed.

The boys stared at each other, with Mac suddenly uncharacteristically quiet. Paul grinnned, took a slug of his beer and said, 'yeah, was a good trip' and giggled quietly. Mac nodded, finding his own bottle intensely interesting.

Jen could imagine what had gone on, and was trying very hard to think of anything that wouldn't let an image sneak into the main viewing room in her mind when Mac reached across and pulled her off the back of the sofa into his lap and kissed her, leaving her in no doubt whatsoever that he was guilty as all hell. He grinned at her. 'My bad old days,' he said. She punched him in the belly, he pretended to feel it. But then he wrapped his arms around her and held her tight. Paul sipped from his beer again, hoping his envy wasn't written across his face.

At the same time, Cassie was braving the crowds to get all her Christmas shopping done in one day as was her ludicrous, chaotic wont.

Since leaving the house a little after eight that morning, she had covered every inch of the city in the ensuing nine-hour spending marathon. As exhausting as it had been, along the way she'd managed some gorgeous shots she knew she would use sooner or later, and was only missing one present, but had a pretty good idea where to go the next morning to get it. She muttered a triumphant expletive at every-one who'd ever mocked her doing everything at the last minute.

Back home, she survived an undignified clamber up the stairs to her hallway and unceremoniously dumped all her bags at her front door. She was leaning against the wall trying to get her breath back as she fumbled in her bag for keys, but the blood was taking its sweet time getting back to her fingers and she swore loudly. She didn't realise anyone had come up the stairs behind her but looked up, hearing someone knock at the door before hers. Cassie watched him for a moment. He was tall, his face mostly swallowed between an oversized fur hat with ear flaps and a bushy brown beard. He was gently shuffling his feet as he raised his hand to knock again.

'You won't get an answer,' Cassie said, making eye contact.

He stared at her, his hand still raised, then looked back at her neighbour's door and knocked again, a little louder this time. Cassie stopped fishing for her keys and massaged her fingers.

'I'm serious,' she grinned, 'no answer.' Then, seeing his badge, 'You're from the drop-in centre?'

He just nodded.

'What happened to Davie?'

'Ah, his knees couldn't take the stairs anymore.

He does the phones now, means he gets to sit down all day. Me, I'm strong as an ox.' He nodded his head at the door. 'Are they out? Away for the holidays? Maybe I should try again tomorrow?'

'Nah,' said Cassie, 'the place is empty. Has been for as long as I've lived here. It's infamous – Davie didn't tell you? He hated even going past the door, used to run.' She shook her head, amused at the memory.

The man cocked his head to one side.

'You really don't know? Oh man. The land-lord told me when I moved in that everyone he's ever shown the apartment to has refused to even step over the threshold. Reckons it's haunted. More like a colossal tax dodge if you ask me. Anyway, one day he showed me and it really did have the freakiest vibe. Eventually he gave up trying to convince people and started using it for storage but I hear stuff in there all the time – you know, wailing, screaming, rattling chains…'

The man's eyes widened.

'I'm kidding,' she laughed. 'I guess apartments are like people, they creak and sigh sometimes.'

'Like Davie's knees?'

'Yeah,' laughed Cassie, 'just like Davie's knees. Anyway, stay there, I've got a bag of stuff for you, if I can get into my damn apartment.' And with that she had a final successful rummage, opened her own door and left all her shopping in the hallway, letting the door slam behind her. The vibration set the man's teeth on edge. He could hear her moving around her hall amidst clattering and muttering until she reappeared, pink in the face, with a bag of old clothes and a desk lamp which he quickly took from her.

As their hands touched, a small high giggle escaped his lips. Cassie took a step backwards, staring at him.

The man giggled again then said, 'I musta looked pretty silly knocking on the door all that time when there's no-one there, eh?'

Cassie relaxed. 'Easy mistake to make,' she smiled, leaning against the wall, 'so when's your next collection?'

'Oh,' he said slowly, not looking at her as he started packing her donations into big red, white and blue striped nylon laundry bags, 'not for a couple of weeks, I guess. Early in January's good for us – lots of unwanted presents.'

'Cool,' said Cassie, 'we're having a massive clear-out at work but we don't really have a shelter nearby, so I'll bring it back here for you.'

'That's generous of you,' said the man, standing. He turned to leave, but hesitated. He turned back.

'Say, could I ask you a favour?'

'Sure,' said Cassie, straightening up with her camera bag, tripod and a dozen bags of shopping.

'Are all these apartments occupied? Davie just told me the address, didn't say how many people I could expect to find. It sure would save me some time…'

Cassie put all the bags down again, except her precious camera bag which she hoisted up onto her shoulder. She waved an arm at the corridor.

'Five apartments on each floor. Down here there's three occupied – one at either end and me in the middle – stops the building falling over,' she grinned but got a blank stare in return. 'The haunted tax dodge and the one on my other side are empty. Great for loud music – no complaining neighbours! Upstairs I think there's a full house and the floor above that, someone moved out last week but I've no idea what's happening with the apartment. Best bet is to check the mail boxes and see who's not picking up, I guess.'

The man nodded slowly, then made eye contact and smiled broadly. 'Thanks,' he said, 'that makes my job a whole lot easier.'

'No problem,' said Cassie, 'see you around.' Then she shuffled the last of her shopping into her dark hallway, letting the door slam a second time.

The man stood very still, staring at Cassie's closed door. Another little giggle escaped him. He took a skeleton key from his jacket pocket and slipped it into the lock on the door to the supposedly haunted apartment. With a minimum of movement he felt it take hold and turn, hearing an imperceptible click as he was granted access.

He found himself in a small vestibule with a locked door on the far wall that even his key couldn't budge. It didn't matter, he didn't need the rest of the apartment. Quickly stowing the bags of donations into an open box by the door, he climbed carefully around the abandoned crates and boxes to the window, finding it sealed shut with paint and grime. Ventilation was going to be an issue. He found no trace of mice or rats and there was warmth from the surrounding apartments and basement.

It was perfect.

I waited a week before following the postman into the lobby.

'Thanks, buddy.'

'No problem.' He looked at me more closely. 'Say, you new here?'

I smiled ruefully and shook my head. 'Just been put back on nights after a three-year break. These hours are killing me. You know how it is…'

He laughed, kindly. 'I surely do. Well, you enjoy your rest – I'll try to shut the door quietly on my way out.'

I returned his smile and headed upstairs, standing on the landing's curve for a few moments to be certain the hallway was empty, then I hurried along to the empty apartment and let myself in.

With the door closed and locked behind me I relaxed, laying my jacket and packed lunch on the grubby wooden crate by the door.

I stepped over the dusty debris to the far wall and set about building a small, simple hide. Getting found here was no big deal; it wouldn't be the first time I'd pretended to be homeless, scared and weak. If you weren't doing any harm, most people would let you be pretty much anywhere. Still, the landlord might not be good people. I gently lifted boxes, separating piles of long-forgotten junk to create a crawl-space with a couple of dust-sheets for a roof and door. It didn't take long and a quick inspection made me feel good – anyone glancing around would see nothing out of place. I placed my coat and food parcel inside for later and let myself out.

My trawl through the floors above was a quick check of door name-plates, most of which I was relieved to see were the stickers or the home-computer print-off of renters. Only two on the top floor had fixed name-plates.

The whole time I was looking around I kept a bundle of fliers in my hand. They were from the shelter and gave details of collection dates and the kind of things that were good to donate, and what the charity did with the money it raised. They were such easy cover.

Skirving was waiting in the foyer when Cassie left one morning. Hearing her coming he busied himself picking up fallen junk mail and dropped newspapers. As Cassie came round the corner, she looked up and saw him.

'Hey…'

Skirving made no attempt to remind her of his name.

'Good morning,' he smiled. 'Want this? It's my last one.'

It wasn't my last one. It was my only one.

Cassie took the flier and glanced through the hand-written scrawl.

'I made them myself. I figured it might help people. You like it?'

Cassie stifled a snort of derision. 'Yeah, it's lovely. And it means I definitely won't miss your next collection – I'll pin it right up on the board in my kitchen so I don't forget.' She shook the flier at him. 'This was a great idea of yours.'

She waved a hand over her shoulder as she walked past him and out into the winter sunshine. On the top step she turned and glanced at Skirving who had his back to her. 'Weirdo,' she muttered, and ran down the steps to the bus stop.

Cassie had tried every excuse in the book to avoid spending the holidays back home but her mom had resorted to what she knew would work. 'Do it for me, if not for you,' she'd said. Cassie had caved.

– Just how the hell did you say no to that and not disappear in a cloud of selfish guilt, she wondered?

What compounded her burgeoning sulk was that she was expected to show up at a pre-Christmas drinks party at Jen's, watching as she and her lovely man played host to some of their school, college and work friends. Cassie was taking refuge at her mom's, being keen to avoid her own apartment. A recent fling had imploded messily the day before, and her shame at explaining the disturbance to the police her neighbours had called in fright was now fading with each glass of red wine. She was dreading having to watch domestic bliss unfold against a backdrop of snow, carols, eggnog and perfect couples as Mac and Jen celebrated their first Christmas together.

On arrival at Jen's, she had taken as much talk of house prices, pregnancies and promotions as she could stand before the numbness started to wear off. Aware that she was being unusually quiet and unwilling to discuss the reasons with anyone, she stomped through to the kitchen and started in on the mulled wine, wishing she wasn't such a cliché.

As she slugged the first couple of mugs back, she thought about her eight months with Luke, which had ended somewhat abruptly less than twenty-four hours ago when he'd admitted, a little sheepishly, that he couldn't spend Christmas with her as he was obliged to spend it with his real girlfriend and their new baby. Without missing a beat, he'd asked her what she was doing for New Year's, which is when Cassie had thrown a pan at him and woken a neighbour's baby as she followed him down the hall and a flight of stairs into the front yard, screaming the entire way in remarkably biological detail just where he should stick it. Back indoors she'd wrenched the cork out the first bottle and in a fit of clarity, resolved to spend the holidays drunk as a skunk with the sole intention of coming up on January 5th with chronic amnesia.

It was as good a plan as any.

People came and went getting beers from the fridge, but Cassie did nothing more than nod and grace a few with a wan smile. She eventually took her fifth mug of Mac's lethal concoction back through to the party and in the dimmed light found herself unable to focus much, which is when she saw him. Well, to be fair, she saw three of him, but if she screwed her eyes tight, she could be fairly sure there was only one, even if he was vibrating at a frequency hitherto unrecognised in humans.

But there he was, just one beautiful man. Wobbling slightly. Had he been there all along? She must be losing her touch.

'You'll do,' she thought, and then realised just how drunk she might be. It was a real effort, concentrating on mapping a path around furniture, tree, boxes, gifts and guests that wouldn't result in her falling flat on her face. Through the wine fog she realised that even if she survived the treacherous crossing uninjured, any kind of coherent speech was probably beyond her. She tried to practise but couldn't find her face. Her lips were out there somewhere, she was sure she'd seen them in the mirror before she came out but now, well who knew where they'd gone?

She tentatively waggled her wine-numbed tongue trying to determine what shape her mouth was, hoping that some random muscle memory would make speech happen. It felt unlikely. She began to think a swiftly downed bucket of mulled wine on top of a day's drinking wasn't so much Dutch Courage as Gross Stupidity.

Cassie heard Jen's voice beside her.

'You drunk?'

'Mmmmf. See…' said Cassie, turning to her and trying to see. 'Thing is, right…thing is…(what was the thing?)…thing is…(oh yeah) thing is, sometimes my heart's in charge, forra bit, and thass lovely, but my heart is super-stupid and when it craps up, my liver's in charge. Fixes everything. See?'

Jen saw. 'It's over? Oh god, Cassie, why didn't you tell me, babe? What the hell happened? I thought you guys were doing so well…'

Cassie could instantly feel self-pity liquidise behind her eyes, and was damned, even in this state, if she'd start crying. It had taken such an effort to stop that to let go now seemed like more failure than even she could stand.

'Already gorra girlfriend, hasn'he? Surpriiiise!' Cassie waved a hand in what she hoped was an urbane, devil-may-care kinda way. Shame it was the hand with the mug in it, really. In mallow-fluff slo-mo she watched a mug's worth of mulled wine arc through the air, threatening to cascade all over Jen's new carpet, so she over-compensated with a step back. Completely unbalanced, she fell over the corner of the table and smacked her head on the sofa arm on the way down. As she fell, mulled wine flew gracefully above her, flooding across the table and dripping off the far side like a Willy Wonka candy waterfall.

'Ooooww and bloody hell and ooowww some

more. What the fuck jus' happened? I'm upside down…'

For a few minutes Cassie tried and failed to prop herself up on one arm, but as Jen helped her sit, she stuck her tongue out and tasted the liquid on the side of her mouth.

'Whass this? Tastes funny…'

'It's blood,' said Jen, concerned. 'You don't remember smacking your head on the way down?'

Mac peered over the back of the sofa, laughing.

'Come on, party girl, let's get you to a bed.'

'Shhhh,' grinned Cassie, 'your girlfriend'll hear us.'

To Cassie's horror, the beautiful man also appeared. He really was very beautiful. She really was very drunk, bleeding and flat on her butt on the floor. 'Here,' he said, 'I'll get this out the way,' and he started mopping the excess wine with a napkin and moving the table to give them all more room.

Cassie looked up at Jen – 'Well, this is dignified' – and then stopped talking as the giddy kicked in and it was all she could do to keep two litres of red wine down.

All three helped drag, push and persuade her through to the spare room where they deposited her on the bed, with Jen pulling off her shoes and rolling the comforter up over her as the boys retreated. Mac nudged Paul, grinned and went back to mingling. In her last moments of consciousness, Cassie looked up at the middle of the beautiful man's three beautiful faces and slurred, 'So you fancy me or what?' and tried to laugh, but when tears came instead she turned her back and promptly passed out.

Cassie dreamed she was sitting cross-legged on the edge of a long, deep pale-tiled channel that disappeared for thousands of miles in each direction. She was beside the middle of three parallel channels, and a bridge to her right allowed you to cross between this and the next and the one behind. The channels were so wide and deep that no matter how hard she looked, there was nothing else to see. In her dream she sat quite calmly, being watched from a far bank by maybe a dozen people, none of whom moved or spoke. Then she began to feel a vibration, one that became a noise, a whisper at first, but building to such a roar that she wondered if she had ever known any other sound. The noise was created by thousands of gallons of dark, tumultuous water rushing in to fill the empty trenches. But they never overflowed, somehow the water level stopped just shy of her and rushed along in furious spate. Near the bridge she became aware of a man standing with his back to her. Without turning around, he executed a perfect dive into the water and she leapt to her feet and threw herself in after him.

The next part of the dream she knew she was far away from where she'd been, but had no recollection of how far or how long she'd travelled, or any memory of her time in the water. Now she stood in a circular white stone space at the foot of a wrought-iron spiral staircase. There were five green-painted wooden doors, just like the ones at home. She opened each in turn and behind each was someone she seemed to recognise but didn't know. All she knew for certain was that they were dead. Each person acknowledged her and went back to what they were doing – the first reading, the second sitting on an upturned metal bucket staring into space, the third curled up ready to doze, the fourth watching her to see what she'd do, and then the last one who stepped out his room and escorted her up the stairs to the street she'd grown up on, except here she knew it was always night. Everything was bathed in dark green light and the cobbled street was deserted apart from a gypsy caravan with no horse to pull it, and the only sign of life a tiny monkey, sat watching her from the abandoned wooden shafts. She felt a gentle push on her back, and went home. And that's when she woke up. Every time. It was a dream she had often, and it never seemed to make much sense, though it always left her feeling melancholy and restless.

It was early afternoon, she was dehydrated and only too aware of her aching bladder. She peeled her tongue off the roof of her mouth and lay for five blissful seconds where she recalled absolutely nothing. From the window she could see just the tips of the dark firs against the grey skyline and a light fall of snow start from the heavy cloud cover. Winter was just the…

Then she remembered.

'Oooooh noooooo,' she moaned, pulling the comforter right up over her face. Sadly, it failed to live up to its name and she lay in the hot dark, cringing as her brain drip-fed her the events of the previous evening. When she remembered her last words to the gorgeous stranger, she sat bolt upright, suddenly wishing she hadn't when sloshing nausea rebounded off the back of her skull and caught up with her eyes.

'No, no, no, no,' she pleaded with herself, but she knew she'd done a Cassie Special, and with witnesses too.

She closed her eyes and breathed. Bad idea. She opened her eyes, tried to focus on a bit of wallpaper pattern, concentrating hard on keeping the contents of her stomach from making an impromptu reappearance.

She thought about the beautiful man and wished herself dead.

– Too late now, she figured. Nice going, idiot.

She drew the blanket back and slowly swung her feet onto the floor, looking across the room expecting to have to stare down the dishevelled lush in the dresser mirror.

Where the hell had her face gone?

It took a few minutes for her remaining brain cells to process that there was a note taped to the glass, right where her head should have been.

She reached across and grabbed it. Sitting back she breathed slowly until she was reasonably sure she wouldn't be sick. Looking down at the note she saw there was writing on it, in genuine hieroglyphics. Right now the world looked like some dreadful seventies K-Tel soft-focus nightmare and rubbing her filthy contacts didn't seem to be helping. She stuck her fingers into the glass of water by the bed, poked liquid in the corners of her eyes and blinked furiously until the letters stopped doing that fuzzy thing and reformed into English.

All that was written on it was 'Yes' and a phone number, and it was signed 'Paul'. She stared at it for a long time, then dropped it on the bed. Looking back at the mirror she saw a blossoming purple smear between her right ear and eye – wild sofas really shouldn't be approached without the appropriate safety equipment, she thought – and was touched to see that Jen (please let it have been Jen) had cleaned and dressed the tiny wound. Cassie decided she'd seen pandas with smaller black circles round their eyes. Also, what was left of her make-up looked like classic Jackson Pollock and, off-set against her grey skin and classic Mad Scientist hair, she really had outdone herself this time. Pointing at her reflection she said, 'I am a goddess, and I deserve a man who will love, value and respect me.' Then she very nearly choked to death laughing.

The laugh was cut short by a burp that required her to swallow a sudden up-rush of bile. It tasted worse than foul and she slugged back some flat water, coughing as she forced it down.

'Morning, sunshine. Feeling better?' asked Jen from the doorway.

'I feel like nine kinds of shit, babe,' spluttered Cassie, 'but a sympathy date is better than no date, right?' and she waved the crumpled note at her best friend.

As standing upright made her queasy, Cassie padded through to the bathroom on all fours and took her shower sitting cross-legged in the bath, letting the water drum on her medicated head until it was time to get vertical which she did clinging to the walls, muttering prayers and apologies to any gods listening.

She feebly dried whatever she could reach without bending, stretching or basically moving much at all, then gingerly made her way to the kitchen, grateful to find that Paul had gone shopping. Cassie endured Mac's sniggering as he cooked her a mountain of bacon and eggs. Keen to be away before Paul's return, she wolfed it down, but still found time and room for two toasted bagels with cream cheese, nearly an entire pot of coffee, three glasses of OJ and most of the candy off the tree.

Mac called her a cab and for the short ride home she lay slumped in back, breathing out loud and massaging her tumultuous belly.

As she let herself into her mom's house, she heard laughter from the front room and Kath came out to meet her in the hall.

'Sissy's here!' she hissed, half-dragging Cassie into the kitchen. 'She even brought her own sherry!'

Noticing the bruise and Band-Aid on her daughter's face she raised an eyebrow. 'Good party?'

'The sofa bit me, mom, that's all.'

Kath, having prepared a guest room for two at the start of the holidays, thought better of asking after Luke, figuring his absence meant he wasn't so different, despite her daughter's protestations. She already knew that men never seemed to last too long, but the defensiveness Cassie could summon when questioned was enough to ruin more than just the day.

As Cassie poured them both some fresh coffee, she said, 'Jen says hey, and she'll be over in the next day or two.'

'That's sweet. How's Mac doing?'

'Ah mom,' said Cassie, sounding just as resigned as she felt, 'the perfect Mac is as perfectly perfect as ever. But you know it's like winning the lottery, right? Once you know someone who wins, you just know you're never gonna…'

Kath paused, trying to figure out a way around the thing neither of them wanted to discuss. She reached over and stroked her daughter's hair. 'I have to go…Sissy'll strip the room…you know what she's like,' Cassie managed a small smile, 'but I want you to think about coming by your grandma's on New Year's. She'd love to see you, you know.'

Cassie sipped her coffee and contemplated her grandma's party – sure it was the single girl's last great refuge to play dutiful daughter and grand-daughter, but she believed in starting the year as you meant to go on. She was horrified at the prospect it might be in a draughty old house full of widows, dribbling spinsters and other assorted borderline schizo relatives.

Apart from anything else, it would doubtless involve her extended family asking why she was alone and when was she going to settle down? Cassie knew that kind of interrogation was entirely incompatible with sobriety, particularly if dealing with her two maiden great-aunts at once. Their persistence could make bloodhounds seem half-assed.

Florrie, the younger of the two at eighty-six, seemed able to answer any question, though sadly never in the order you asked them. With her a conversation, if it could be called that, was like trying to do a jigsaw in the dark, blindfold, without the benefit of the original picture and quite possibly with both hands tied behind your back. Everything would be accompanied by vacant grinning and a great deal of over-enthusiastic nodding, which often required the rescue of her teeth from some dusty corner.

'Would you like some soup, Florrie?'

'My back's gone again. Doctor says I've not to sneeze.'

'Have you been out much, Florrie?'

'A small sherry, if you're having one yourself. Just for medicinal, if you know what I mean...'

'How do you take your tea, Florrie?'

'See, I stick it through the bigger hole and just hope it doesn't fall out when I'm not looking, ha ha.'

And so it went on.

Sissy was her elder, indomitable ninety-two-year-old sister and easily the maddest of Cassie's mad aunts. As a kid, Cassie had always been fascinated by her lazy left eye which verged on apathetic given she could practically see inside one of her own ears.

Sissy had apparently spent her adolescence refining her kleptomaniac tendencies, working in the finer hotels of Western Europe. These days she seemed unable to restrain her inner cuckoo and now nothing was safe unless nailed down. And even then probably not. Her favourite thing was to take her napkin at dinner and fold it when she thought no-one was looking, one fold at a time, closer and closer to the edge of the table. With each fold it acquired a piece of cutlery and eventually she'd fold the clanking bundle into her handbag, all the while grinning madly at the assembled family and thinking herself the best in the business.

It had always been Cassie's job as a kid to wait for Sissy to 'pop off for a quick yes-yes' and rescue the family silver from her cavernous handbag while she was otherwise occupied.

And then there was her beloved grandma, who would pat her on the knee and say how beautiful she'd look in white, and where was the Prince Charming for her only princess? Followed by a sigh, and a 'How hard could it be to find a nice boy, now that she wasn't getting any younger and really, it was high time to start a family of her own and she couldn't be Calamity-Cassie for ever…'

The thought of trying to explain to the three of them, sober, why she'd come home for the holidays unaccompanied was unthinkable.

Cassie turned Paul's note over and over in her pocket.

'Maybe, mom, I'll let you know.'

At that moment, Sissy appeared in the kitchen doorway, a huge glass of sweet sherry in one hand and a thick pile of old family photos in the other.

'Just look at your face!' grinned Sissy, throwing the photos onto the counter and squeezing Cassie's cheek. 'Has poor Calamity-Cassie had an unhappy love affair?' Cassie wasn't sure whether to laugh, cry or punch the bitch.

'Is there any other fucking kind?' she muttered and slunk out the room.

There's no day so bad that it can't get slightly worse.

In the garden she choked back tears, wondering whether she was heartbroken, ashamed, livid or all of the above.

She climbed over the fence and slumped down onto a damp rock by the Holliers' pond, poked the gelatinous surface with a twig and wondered if she stood a chance of ever evolving. Her love affair hadn't been unhappy. On the contrary. The sex had been sublime, she'd laughed a lot, accepted some wonderful gifts and been eaten in some fine hotels. The only real down side was that being given a cell number meant she wasn't welcome to call Luke at work or home. Of course, they had never spent one whole night together. Cassie had chosen not to think about it all too much, reminding herself frequently that she was single, and therefore not doing anything wrong.

In truth, she'd been pretty much untroubled by anything approaching morality and had thrived on it all, discovering that she seemed to do more productive and creative work when behaving like an accomplished tart.

The logistics of duplicity came easily to Cassie and the only part that really bothered her was that affairs so depressingly easy to get into were invariably so ugly to leave. It wasn't as if she expected or even wanted a real relationship, having proved to herself over and over again that she was perfect mistress material.

For a game she was used to winning, her ego hurt when caught out like this. The rules were simple. How could she have been so easily fooled? She knew she was the quick fix fuck. She would be the spontaneous passion that no longer existed because it had been replaced with something deeper and more meaning-ful. She was the adolescent thrill, the cheap drug, the disposable whore to remind them how they'd got to where they were now. She was flashback. She was the surprise erotic dream on a dull Tuesday afternoon. It had nothing to do with her.

The novelty of being the novelty soon wore off but as it did she would always find a way to escape with her ego intact. This time, Luke had changed the rules.

What was making her angriest was that she should have seen it coming and pre-empted him, but she'd been so caught up in the season that she'd left herself vulnerable. It was impossible not to. For weeks the entire city had been trapped beneath thick dove-grey cloud that shook snow on buildings, trees and people. There was nothing for it but to wrap up and go out and play, either skating on the outdoor rink or gig-gling like six-year-olds on the carousel in the park. The best evenings were rare ones when they went back to hers, shook off their layers and lay curled on the sofa. Candles and dancing lights lit every window, her Christmas tree sagged under the weight of candy and tinsel and every screen or print image she saw was of some blissfully happy couple, lounging by an open fire, their season peppered with kisses and gifts, champagne and time.

She knew in her needy little mind that she'd super-imposed them both onto any and all of these images, simply editing out his real life. What did she really think was going to happen? She didn't actually want him, not really, but her only real thrill was to lever things to the point where something exciting might happen.

'Yeah,' she thought, idly chipping away at a stubborn icicle, 'I'm such a class act.'

The very worst thing about it all was having no-one else to blame.

With Cassie gone, Jen made a fresh pot of coffee and when Paul returned, all three of them stood in the living room doorway, each nursing a steaming mug, staring at the post-party devastation.

'Ugh,' said Jen, 'this is the bit I hate.'

'Yeah,' said Mac, sinking down onto the sofa, 'but it won't take you too long, right, babe?'

Jen lobbed a scrunched up ball of wrapping paper at him. He grinned and started gathering up the debris around his feet. Paul fetched a refuse sack from the kitchen as well as a tray and Jen started collecting dirty glasses.

It took maybe an hour, complete with Mac insisting on stripping to his shorts and playing Queen's *I Want to Break Free* while he ran the vacuum round the room. Jen sat on the sofa in fits of giggles and Paul took the opportunity to sneak out into the back yard and enjoy the late afternoon chill. He didn't hear Jen come outside, but he was grateful for the blanket. Once he'd wrapped it round his shoulders, she handed him a fresh coffee.

'I love this time of day,' he said, 'the sun's gone but it's like the world holds its breath, delaying the dark just as long as it can stand. Like someone pressed the pause button on the world. It's like a tiny gift from the gods to let you catch up and figure some shit out.'

Jen sipped her coffee and waited.

'So that's Cassie, huh?'

'Yep,' said Jen, staring straight ahead at the row of firs at the end of the far field. She had an urge to tell Paul that Cassie was bad news, that she never really loved anyone, that she did things because she could, that she would just take whatever he could give her and then be gone. But there was something about Paul that stopped her. He hadn't responded to Cassie the way most men did, 'Cats like you, right?' she asked.

Paul laughed and blew on his coffee, his hands wrapped around the mug.

'Yeah,' he laughed, 'I'm stupidly allergic, but they don't give a shit…they always seem to want to talk to me.'

Jen just nodded.

Paul opened his mouth to say something, but hesitated. He tried again. Jen waited.

'Do you think she'll call me?'

Jen's laugh was hollow. 'Oh, she'll call.'

The sky was still a perfect colour-match for Cassie's hungover skin, but after just a light flutter, the snow had stopped falling as if even gravity was too much like hard work. She took her coffee to the end of their back garden and using the lowest branch, stepped up onto the last remaining platform of her old tree-house.

'Thanks, dad,' she whispered, kissing her name where he'd carved it out the trunk, and she drew her knees to her body, hugging herself tight with her feet resting against the trunk. Looking down she tried to remember how a few feet from the ground used to feel like miles; how frightened she'd been when her dad had lifted her from his shoulders and deposited her there for the first time. She'd laughed to show how brave she was, but reached for him all the same and he'd lifted her straight back down again. Of course, by the time Jen saw it, Cassie could scamper up there without hesitation, and she shook her head, smiling ruefully as she recalled the unforgivably hard time she'd given Jen for being too chicken to join her.

She missed those days. Those were days that ended being tucked into a cosy bed, days that ended with a story and the sweetest kiss. These days she felt like she was on a fairground ride where the carney mistook her screams for laughter and spun her harder. She had a sneaking suspicion that the ride didn't stop of its own volition and she would have to be flung out for things to stop.

She finished her coffee and, putting the mug down, breathed into her hands and rubbed them together. When she could feel her fingers properly, she took out her cell and Paul's note, and sat holding both, just watching the house and the sky.

She considered going to get a beer – an entirely justifiable hair of the dog – but decided in a moment of mature reflection that perhaps one whole sober day wouldn't hurt. More to the point, just thinking about the smell of it made her stomach spasm.

She opened up Paul's note and decided she liked his handwriting. 'Please let him be a decent human being,' she mumbled, all the while hoping fervently that Luke was bloody miserable.

She dialled.

It rang once, twice, three…four…five times.

'Ah, thank Jesus,' she exhaled, about to hang up just as a honey voice said, 'Paul speaking.'

Cassie's voice sealed up.

'Hello? Cassie?'

She squeaked.

'How's your hangover?' he asked, the smile audible in his voice.

She drew a breath.

'Oh, you know, thriving, thanks. Just like the embarrassment, shame and bruising.'

He laughed outright. It was a good laugh and Cassie, all by herself in a tree, grinned.

'So,' he started, faltering only a little, 'can I… ah…can I buy you dinner?'

'That depends,' she retorted, instantly defensive. 'Are you married? Do you have enough kids to fill two station wagons? Do whole clubs of strippers know you by name? What does your boyfriend do? What are your prospects? Do you ever wear your mother's underwear? What were you in prison for? Do you love hockey more than women? Do you now or have you ever practised Magik-with-a-K? Do you still live in your parents' basement? Do you…'

He interrupted her when she drew breath.

'Relax, Cassandra, it's only dinner.'

Cassie bristled. 'Jen told you never to call me that, right?'

'Uh-huh,' he said, 'which means you're gonna have to stick around long enough to see if I do as I'm told.'

'Just dinner?' she asked
'Just dinner,' he said, softly.
'What…no sex?'

# Chapter Fourteen

Whenever your love life's in a mess, people always tell you to move on. So I did. North, again, stopping on the East coast a little shy of Washington.

The entire episode with Emily had given me renewed hope and plenty of ideas, and now more than anything I wanted another chance. I was hungry to prove myself. I knew now that the right woman would save me. Redeem me. Elevate me.

I did a little manual work, made a little cash, hung out for a while. Most days I just liked to drive around, see what I could see.

After a couple of weeks Rachel is what I saw. There were maybe two or three girls each day that I thought were pretty close to Emily, but with Rachel it was more than that. Sure, she really caught my eye but as I sat at the edge of a parking lot with the engine idling, she turned left coming out a store next door and at that exact moment, the left filter light came on so I could keep tailing her. The sign was a sign!

I followed her home, then left the car in a supermarket lot a block away, took my toolbox and went to check out her building. Poor Rachel. She was as lonely as me, all alone in a crumbling old block. I had to wait till I saw her at a window till I could figure out which apartment she had, then I stopped by and told her the condo manager had hired me to work through a list of repairs; told her I was there to do whatever needed doing. She seemed a little cool at first but then her cat came padding to the door and rubbed itself all over my good jeans, mewing and pushing against my ankles. She said if Tabitha liked me, I couldn't be all bad.

Turned out her apartment really needed some fixing. Lucky old me, I'm good with stuff like that. Women are always so glad to find a guy who can turn his hand to pretty much anything.

Me and Rachel, we got to be friends. I found myself telling her some true things about me, about when I'd worked for a cobbler, a locksmith, even a baker who taught me how to make perfect donuts. She thought it sounded romantic, having so many jobs. Because things didn't work out so well last time, I was super-careful. I already knew we were right for each other, but by then I had learned to show just a little bit at a time.

The biggest problem with Emily, eventually, was she didn't understand that some things are good to hear, you know? Even the worst day can be wiped away by someone saying just the right thing to you. Sometimes you just need to hear words that make you feel appreciated. Emily seemed to think it was a game and whenever I tried to make her say something, she would back off, like it was funny to make me wait. Well, this time I figured that was the one problem needing fixed more than anything else.

To start with it was all good, it was all just fine. I could say one thing and it would make Rachel say the right thing back at me. I really liked that when it worked. I even had fun experimenting to see just how far I could take it. Rachel was pretty responsive but mostly because she was a little bit sweet on me. That helped.

After a little while I guess maybe I got greedy, wanting to hear too much too soon but that's not my fault. Anyone would have felt the same way. Things were going so well I just wanted everything to be perfect. I guess I got a little ahead of myself. I've always been pretty impulsive. If I think of something good, I just want it straight away. Waiting takes the fun out of everything.

Soon, things got kinda unpredictable. Even with the most unsubtle prompting, the things she was saying were ludicrous and irrelevant. She wouldn't respond to what should have been foolproof stimuli. It was clear she wasn't taking our relationship seriously.

When it became obvious that things were not going to go my way I realised she had left me little choice. I knew then that my next ideal woman would take a little more time and planning if I was going to get her right, so I wanted to make a fresh start as soon as possible.

It's hard to know what a lethal dose is. I mean, people are all so different, you know?

Rachel invited me over one afternoon, asking me to help her clear out the little garden out back. I showed up with a bottle of home-made smoothie as a gift.

The afternoon's work was back-breaking and repetitive. I didn't mind. The day was going to be so special. It only took us a few hours to clear away all the junk and uproot most of the weeds. She seemed so happy out there, I was actually starting to feel real sorry things weren't going to end well for her.

Back inside I took the smoothie from the fridge and poured it all out.

'You're not having any?'

I smiled at her. 'Can't. Allergic to strawberries, but I know they're your favourite.'

She blushed a little at this. She was cute when she blushed. I took another bottle from my bag.

'I made myself a mango one. Cheers.'

We both drank.

At first she screwed up her face a little but I laughed and gently reassured her.

'My granny's secret ingredient. She swears it keeps summer colds at bay.'

Rachel just grinned and took two long drinks,

almost finishing it.

'My granny had a…'

But then she stopped talking. Her glass was almost empty and her face was a strange colour. I stepped forward in time, catching the tumbler just as it started to slip from her slack hand.

I watched her crumple to the floor, her legs giving way under her like the bones had melted.

I stepped around her, careful not to touch any part of her. A light came to her eyes as the last of her consciousness flared briefly, and then they rolled back in her head exposing the whites as the seizures engulfed her. Rachel.

Frustrating how someone who looked so right could have been so wrong.

Poor Rachel.

I dosed the bitch.

I stayed long enough to make sure she'd ingested enough to kill her. I watched as she chewed her tongue into a ragged pulp, bits of torn flesh bubbling from her mouth in a scarlet froth. Her entire body convulsed into grotesque contortions like a marionette in the hands of a clumsy child…I couldn't have made her twitch any harder if I'd taken my Taser to her.

After that, if she didn't drown in her own blood, she would never recover from the coma. I have no idea which it was in the end, because I had a Greyhound to catch.

# Chapter Fifteen

Cassie decided she was long overdue for a day in the office. She had no choice. She was fresh out of coffee, staples and toilet roll.

Working from home had made her lazy and although she'd had every intention of being in first thing – 10 a.m., give or take – by the time she sifted through the piles of debris that obscured her desk (she was never deluded enough to call it a work station), it was gone eleven.

Once across town, what little remained of her morning passed with a series of petty layout arguments with Gordon, too much coffee and as much flirting with the male staff as she could fit in. She declined a series of lunch offers, knowing that the abandoned space would give her plenty of time to restock the kitchen, office and bathroom of her tiny apartment.

By the time 1 p.m. rolled around, she and a sullen middle-aged temp called Pam were the only ones left and Cassie's bag was groaning with 'perks'.

She settled down to deal with old email – which was when Pam decided to start sharing. Within half an hour, Cassie had more intimate knowledge of the workings of Pam's bladder than she could ever have imagined, the mere mention of her pee being green some mornings putting her right off her lunch. She went to make more coffee.

'Too much coffee gives you cystitis…'

Cassie sat down and jabbed at her phone, speed-dialling Jen. When she'd caught up on a week's worth of gossip, she lingered over the grisly details of her previous weekend's encounters and promised vaguely, yet again, that this weekend would be different.

Call over, she highlighted what was more than a week old in her inbox and pressed the 'delete' key.

'There', she said, pleased with herself. 'That's my email dealt with.' She winked at the truculent Pam whose only response was to lean over the low parti-tion and viciously hiss at Cassie, 'You know you'll never find a man good enough for you, don't you?''

That was something of a slap in the face at half past one on a wet Friday afternoon, but Cassie was unsure how to respond. She sipped at her cold coffee, took a deep breath and moved her chair back a little so she wouldn't get caught in the blast radius if a passing tornado happened to drop a house on the witch.

Not another word was uttered between them

that afternoon but the fact that to date the god-awful woman had been right bothered Cassie for the rest of the day. She stared at her monitor, seeing nothing, turning Pam's words over and over in her mind.

Her mood didn't lift when she quit for the evening, although she was delighted to discover as she left that Pam wouldn't be back. She still felt weird through the first three beers in her local where she sat slumped against the bar, growling quietly. She was surrounded by happy-hour office parties celebrating the end of yet another week of meaningless grind. Bilious and feeling conspicuous, she opened a news-paper lying nearby and laid her cell phone in front of her, hoping against hope that someone would call and make her look less abandoned. Worried that the first three beers might be lonely, she started supplying them with a wide social network.

Staggering home a little after midnight, all she could focus on was trying not to crash into other drunk women staggering about from bar to bar, all of whom, without exception, Cassie thought, were dressed like the worst kind of trashy movie hookers.

'You all look like whores. But not good trashy movie whores, oh no. Not Jamie Lee Curtis in *Trading Places* for you, you skanks, all good skin and bright eyes cos a lifetime of personal trainers and a macro-biotic diet can't be disguised by a spangly boob-tube and some red lippy. You all look like street-walkers, god help you.'

Cassie swivelled to see their view from behind as they went up the steps into a club. It wasn't good.

'Great,' she muttered, 'I could have done without that.'

She looked up at the bouncer who seemed to have a blind spot. Cassie ducked and bobbed around a bit trying to catch his eye but it made her dizzy.

'I used to go on holiday to France', she slurred 'and every year I'd have to go to a Bastille Day barbecue and they'd have these totally gross sausages called andouillettes which is a big white bag of lumpy gristle an' when they grilled it, the skin split and bubbling white meat and little multi-coloured mysteries came bursting right out and they looked exactly like waterlogged corpses exploding.'

The bouncer finally stared down at her with an expression that suggested he wasn't getting paid enough to be accosted by drunk women shouting about sausages.

'An' these women,' Cassie waved her hand in the general direction of the club's entrance, 'what they don' know is that from the back they look a hell of a lot like French sausages.'

Just then, another party of girls appeared outside the club and started their pre-mating ritual with some guys across the street. Cassie stopped and stared. The tallest of the girls wore a very short black simple dress. She had glossy hair, bare tanned legs that went on for forever and she was beautiful. Cassie hated her. But not for long. The woman stuck two fingers in her mouth and whistled shrilly, ensuring she had not only the guys' attention but pretty much everyone on the entire block, then she turned her back on them, bent forward and lifted the back of her dress, flashing her perfect ass. Done, she clapped her hands, squealed and ran around high-fiving her girlfriends. Then, just in case the guys had forgotten her, she did it all again.

Cassie watched the whooping tribe across the street applaud the women and decided that they were idiots. She made a brief mental note to start drinking in a classier part of the city and then went back to hoping, vehemently, that they would all die. In pain. Alone. She supposed it was too much to expect them to do it quietly.

She looked up at the bouncer who was unsubtly shifting his position, hoping Cassie would get the hint. She did and it made her want to cry.

'S'alright. Don' wanna come in. Wanna kill someone. See ya.'

Cassie was angry but not the really useful kind of angry where she could scream and shout or smash things. This was the kind of angry that made her physically vibrate until she thought she might burst something. Redundant, negative energy pulsed through her, making her want to ricochet off the walls, fizzing, livid and reaching critical mass with surplus fury.

'If I drink fast and hard enough,' she figured, 'my brain will melt and cave in. And then I'll be able to fast-track to self-pity, weeping and, hopefully, bliss-ful unconsciousness which means I get to wake up tomorrow morning feeling stupid, marginally more resolved and prepared for a teeny tiny fresh start.'

Cassie found a cab and having promised she wouldn't throw up, got it to take her to the one place she figured might make it all OK.

Having made it to Carnegie's in one piece she deposited her keys and jacket with Toby behind the bar. He motioned Cassie to a stool nearer the end of the bar but thought better of asking her what was wrong. He was used to being her confidante, confes-sor, scratching post or big brother, depending on the passing crisis, and wondered, briefly, if he'd ever be sure that asking her on a date was a smart move.

Cassie loved Carnegie's. It was a cool, quiet, rela-tively small place with a little TV above the bar and some faded sports photographs on the walls. There were wooden tables and chairs, and in back some leather-upholstered booths and a purple pool table in need of a shave. A rack of newspapers by the door and some of the best spicy fries in town made it her home from home. She mooched by here at least three times a week and at some point every weekend when, even on a Saturday night, it was never too crazy.

Without waiting to be told, he put a glass in front of her, added some ice and poured a shot of her favourite vodka. She drained it, letting the cool of the ice rest against her lips. With the glass safely back on the bar he shook his head at her raised eyebrows and replaced it with a taller glass with more ice and a mixer. She and Toby knew this routine by heart.

'All right darling,' she slurred, 'keep 'em coming till I'm dead.'

Toby gave her one of his best disapproving looks which Cassie got into focus in less than a minute. 'Ah, man, it's OK. I promise not to start anything or bite anyone or cry or pass out in the bathroom.'

Within the hour she was slumped face down on the wooden bar wondering just how close she was to drinking herself sober. She wasn't. The only thing she was totally sure of was that there was just no way she could drink this mood into submission on her own.

A half hour and two drinks later she was no less angry but a whole lot more drunk. A group of seven guys had arrived and were stood around her at the bar.

Cassie didn't recognise them but soon after they got settled, one started talking to her and it had been the second maternal warning glance from Toby that had made her belligerent enough to flirt right back. The stranger bought her a drink and she'd finally decided, when they announced they were going clubbing and invited her along, that maybe dancing would succeed where drinking had failed. She loved to dance. She would dance this goddamn mood into the ground.

She'd watched Toby check with the guys where they were going and resented his interfering. As she left with seven strangers, she said to him, 'So when they find my raped corpse in a ditch, you'll be the expert witness, huh?' Her laugh sounded hollow to both of them. 'I'll be fine, Toby – we're only going to RedEye.'

'OK Cassie,' he said, 'but just take it easy, please hon?' He passed her belongings across the bar.

Cassie nodded glumly, poked the slice of lime around her vodka, licked her finger and slugged the fresh drink back in one.

RedEye was one of Cassie's regular clubs. The owner was an old school friend and not only was she guest-listed for life but the six regular bouncers all knew her by name. She assumed that when they checked in with her as they made their rounds of the dance floor, it was because they were looking out for her. As she was fond of telling Jen, it really always was all about her. It had never occurred to her that they might be making sure she wasn't getting in too much of the wrong kind of trouble. Still, she always felt safe at RedEye and if she'd been able to face speaking in sentences, she'd have reminded Toby of just that.

When she arrived at the club, she was waived straight through and ran for the dance floor, not waiting for her new friends to pay. Ten minutes later she felt hands on her hips and opened her eyes to see the cute guy from Carnegie's smiling as he held out a drink for her. She grinned and grabbed it from him, then he took her by the hand and led her to a dark corner, but on the way she didn't see any of his friends around.

He gently pressed her back against the wall and started kissing her. Cassie closed her eyes, content to let him. The music held her up and she let the pounding rhythms talk to the unsettled bits of her, hoping that she would soon find a rhythm of her own.

It didn't happen.

The guy, whose name she would never find out, didn't seem aware or bothered that her responses were non-existent. His hands slid under her shirt, his ineffectual kisses wet her face, but Cassie was numb. She sank back inside herself, as once more the tiniest Russian Doll drowned in the darkness. It didn't matter what her shell did any more; she couldn't feel a thing.

A quiet voice inside her reasoned that if she couldn't drink or dance this mood out her system, maybe she needed to fuck it away. When she made her thinking clear, there was no objection from the stranger.

Leaving the club he told her which hotel he was staying in, admitting he had no idea how to get there from here. Cassie's heart sank. It was the other side of town and cabs were pretty thin on the ground round this neighbourhood. Then she had a stroke of genius. The hotel chain had a sister two blocks away at the Lake and Cassie led them that way. On arrival, she told the concierge they were staying in the main hotel and he arranged a courtesy driver to take them back. Cassie felt psyched, like she was surfing the entire evening.

By the time they were in his room she had begun to sober up – the lights were too bright; his luggage was spilled all over the floor; the remains of room service lay half-eaten on a tray and there was a small pile of empty beer bottles by the bed. While he went to the bathroom, she sat on the end of the bed to take off her boots. Looking up to check herself out in the full-length mirror, the woman she saw was waxy-skinned with dark bags under her smudged and tired eyes and an expression that was nothing short of con-temptuous of someone stupid enough to do this, to be in a total stranger's room at 4 a.m. with the dumb plan of screwing a bad mood away. Cassie started to cry.

When he came out, he sat next to her on the bed, putting his arm around her. She felt even worse that he was being nice to her and found herself saying something she never thought she'd hear from her own lips.

'I'm so sorry. I can't do this. I know I've led you on and I feel so bad because I really did mean to go through with this, but I can't. Please understand, I totally didn't mean to mess you about. I have to go.' She pulled her boots back on.

He stood up and went to the door. Cassie rose, then he turned to face her. 'The door's locked.'

Panic surged through her, though her only clear thought was – so do what you have to do to me, but don't hurt me.

It felt like a very long time passed. She couldn't read the expression on his face and, frozen to the spot, she listened to her heart pound, wondering just what the hell happened next.

'Damn,' he said finally, 'where did I throw the key?' and then Cassie started to cry again, though this time with relief.

He unlocked the door and came back to her side.

'You won't stay? We could just curl up together, go to sleep. I'd like that. Please.' And there was something about the way he said it that made Cassie realise she wasn't the only one who had no idea what they were doing.

'I can't', she said, moving around him so he was no longer between her and the door. 'Really, I just can't.' Then she left.

Rather than wait for the elevator, she flew down eight flights, through the foyer and out into the dawn. She ran most of the way home, shaking, tears streaking down her face.

Later, showered and calmer, she reflected that there was nothing quite like real fear to knock a mood on the head. How could she have put herself in such a position? She didn't deserve to be home safe, she knew that, and so notched up one more night when she cried herself to sleep.

# Chapter Sixteen

It seemed each time I moved a little further North, I got closer to what I needed most. In New York my luck showed no sign of running out because there was Nell. The beautiful, perfect Nell. Right from the second I saw her I had those butterflies in my stomach that told me something really special was happening. No more disappointments, I just knew it, because she took me by surprise, pretty much, and it was effortless from that first smile.

I wanted so badly for it all to work out and it seemed like it would. Everything she did, everything she said…I loved everything about her. I was jumpy because I could finally feel it all within my grasp; this time everything was right. I could feel it. Shauna would have been so proud, so happy for me.

With Emily it all went wrong after a month; Rachel nearly three months, but with Nell it showed no sign of stopping. To begin with I was kinda afraid that she would do something wrong, that she'd leave me no choice but to end it all again, but instead she kept surprising me.

She passed every test as if she had done it all a thousand times before.

Nell was the one.

The happier Nell made me, the more I thought about the last couple of years.

I mean, the loss I felt over Shauna kinda blinded me to a lot of things. Emily was a nice idea but I hadn't really thought things through. Finishing things with her felt pretty good at the time because I was finally taking control of my life again and going for what I wanted, what I knew I deserved. I couldn't just settle for something convenient, it had to be right. It had to be perfect. It wasn't until much later that I thought that maybe I'd not really given Emily much of a chance. I guess I kinda over-reacted.

Still, I tried even harder with Rachel. I had to, you know? Not just to get it right but as a belated apology to Emily. I had to get it right for all three of us, and I guess for Shauna too. With Rachel I took time to make a list of all the mistakes I had made with Emily, then made damn sure that I got every single one of those things right second time around. Did she notice? Did she see how much of an effort I was making? Did she ever, even once, reward me for it? Did she hell. It was all Emily's fault that I was trying so damn hard in the first place. Fucking Emily. Just thinking about her got me so mad I had to finish things with Rachel. It wasn't really working out anyway.

And then Nell. With Nell I began to relax.

I should have known better. You can never relax, because there is always something you don't know about waiting to ruin things for you. Sometimes it'll ruin your coffee, sometimes your day, sometimes your whole goddamn life.

One morning Nell called me on her way to work, asked if I would meet her for lunch. From the tone of her voice I knew all my plans were about to change. I took my map from the glove compartment and started plotting a route North.

Later that day she explained how some dumb charity she applied to for teaching overseas had accepted her application, offered her six months in Africa. She was thrilled. Explained how long she'd waited to do this. She couldn't believe she'd met me at the wrong time and asked me to wait for her. I kissed her by way of an answer, but she tasted foul to me. The fact that she could stand to be without me for so long let me see her for what she really was.

We had a month before she would turn her back on me, so she decided to plan a special farewell weekend together when her room-mate would be out of town and we'd have a chance to say goodbye properly.

# Chapter Seventeen

By late January, Cassie figured she should get some work done. She started by muttering furiously to herself as she stomped around the room, growling at her desk and the boxes of files and stacks of CDs sent over from the office.

Having been granted a short extension on a major assignment she'd been too drunk, suddenly single and sulking to contemplate over the holidays, the first two months of Cassie's new year were for work, work and more work. There were hundreds of photographs yet to be sorted, still more to be developed and she had an expanding list of shots she hadn't taken yet.

Her date with Paul was less than a week away but she found herself deeply uncomfortable with the entire situation. Men didn't ask Cassie out on dates; she got drunk and took them home. That's how it had been for so long she couldn't remember if it had really ever been different. On the rare, early occasions when someone had mustered the courage to ask her, she'd been riddled with suspicion. It was probably a joke. A dare.

She called Paul with every intention of cancelling, but hadn't been smart enough to think up a good excuse before dialling.

'Paul? Cassie.'

'Hey, I'm glad you called. How are you?'

'Swamped. Just a crazy amount of work. I have this stupid project I should have finished in December and I've already had my one extension so I've kinda got to get it finished. I'm really sorry – I just don't think I can make this weekend.'

There was the smallest pause, and Cassie simultaneously felt bad about letting him down and elated at being so close to being off the hook.

'What a rough way to start the year! Listen, it's really no problem – I so know what it's like. I have to be away over the first week of February,' there was a pause, 'what about the 12th instead?'

Cassie opened her mouth to protest but all that came out was, 'Sure. 12th it is. Thanks. See you soon.'

She hung up. Put her cell down on the bed. Stared at it. That really wasn't what she'd meant to say. 'Oh,' she said to the room, 'he's willing to wait a couple weeks to buy me dinner. What a loser.'

**That's not very nice.**

She mooched through to her desk, tipped all the boxes out onto the floor and started arranging everything into nice, haphazard piles, then got bored and went to make herself a coffee. Once back, she dug out the source disk, put it in the drive, sat back into her huge ergonomic chair, rested her feet on top of some old files and brought an image up on screen. She stared at it for half an hour while her coffee went cold.

'More coffee.'

**You drink too much coffee.**

Her second cup cooled while she printed off the image and spent twenty minutes drawing moustaches, glasses and fangs on the assembled company. She tacked the much-improved image on the wall by her monitor and kicked back, feet up on the desk and sipped at her now cold coffee.

'Eeww. More coffee.' She went to make a fresh one.

Back at her PC she noticed it was lunchtime.

As the sun started to go down, everyone in the group photo had pointy jester shoes with bells on, giant hairy warts on their noses and sticky-up cartoon hair. Cassie's fingers were covered in daubs from various coloured marker pens and she was very pleased with the way it had turned out, although reasonably sure that the staff of Green Pastures Retirement Home who had employed her agency to design and produce their new brochure wouldn't be quite so chuffed.

It was nearly dark outside. Cassie was bored. She flung her swivel chair around and staggered clumsily out of it across her bedroom, wrenched the wardrobe doors open and stared at the contents.

'I have nothing to wear.'

**You should go shopping.**

She sat on the edge of the bed and called Jen.

'Hi. I am working. Ish. But you know, it's January and I hate my job and I'm broke and bored. God I am so bored. But, you know, blah blah blah. I have nothing to wear. And before you offer, you have nothing I want to wear either. I want to go shopping.'

'I'm up to my neck in it here, Cassie. I have so much to do.'

'Oh really? Oh. I didn't realise you were so busy. Hmm. I guess January must be a pretty busy time for you. I forgot. How about tomorrow afternoon?'

When Jen suggested late-night shopping at the end of the week, Cassie was deliberately petulant about the time and place Jen wanted to meet, eventually breaking her resolve and persuading her they should meet somewhere more convenient for Cassie. Even with her petty victory she still hung up in a sulk.

'I wanted to go now,' she grumbled aloud, slouching back to her desk.

After one hundred and seventeen games of Solitaire, she called it a day.

# Chapter Eighteen

I had two days, so I went to your favourite boutique and looked all over for something I'd like to see you in. There was so much choice, but I knew that trawling always brought the right women to me and I figured if I kept looking, the principle would work with pretty much anything else.

After a little while, an assistant came to harass me – I could tell she was freaked that I was spending so long amongst women's clothes, but I blushed when she spoke to me and told her I was shopping for a present for my sister, something special for my special girl. She was so helpful then, encouraging me to touch fabrics, telling me how refreshing it was to find a man willing to think beyond the clichéd presents women usually get. She complimented me on my good taste. She was flirting with me, but she was wasting her time. Things feel so different now – I mean, when I was alone, every encounter had the potential to be 'the one' but as soon as I found her, my soul-mate-to-be, it's like the lights went out on everyone else. There's not another woman in the world for me any more. She is all there is.

With her help I saw something in your colour. It's a little dressy for a first date but it's stunning. I would love to see you in it. I saw plenty of other stuff, too, so whatever you go for, I'll probably like it. It's easy, because you're so shallow. I know you'll go for distraction. You'll over-compensate. You'll want to show off.

'Too fussy.'

'This?'

'Too pink.'

'This?'

'Too long.'

'This?'

'Too black.'

'This?'

'Too you.'

'Cassie, if you need me, I'll be slumped face down on the floor crying. You are a nightmare.' Jen leant against the wall, folded her arms and stared at her. 'Do you have any idea what you actually want? Ever?'

Cassie glared at her. 'Of course I do! I want something simple but stunning, something elegant and classy. Something...oh fuck, all right, I have no idea. Just something. How about these?'

She held up a pair of black pants, and Jen snorted. 'Those are the ones I pointed at two minutes ago and you said they were too black.'

Cassie passed them to Jen anyway, who draped them over an arm already obscured by various tops and pants.

**Really? You like those?**

Cassie pulled a face. 'OK, so maybe I am being a bit vague. I have no idea what to wear. Remember, the one time I met him I was upside down, bleeding and drunk. Between that and a stressful phone call, it doesn't give me much of a clue.'

Jen grinned at her. 'You have no idea, you know that Cassie? Who cares what he's like? Wear something that makes you happy. Guys like it when a girl's happy. The two of you already fancy each other, so don't beat yourself up over this. You're being ridiculous.'

'What's he like?'

'Paul?'

'No, the baby Jesus you idiot. Of course Paul!'

'He's…nice.' Cassie pulled another face. 'Nice doesn't mean boring, Cassie. He's sweet. Gentle. He's really considerate, too. All through the holidays he wouldn't let me carry any shopping, he helped out around the house. And he's funny. He can be kinda quiet sometimes, but I like that.'

Cassie nodded. 'Did he ever say anything about ex-girlfriends?'

It was Jen's turn to pull a face. 'I really don't know. He and Mac were catching up one night and I was kinda listening in from the study, but I didn't hear much.'

The girls were drifting through the rails of clothes with Cassie's fingers trailing along, not really registering anything when suddenly she grabbed a hanger from the rail.

'What about this?'

**Good girl.**

Jen stared. 'It looks like an explosion in a bowl of spaghetti. Is that a dress?'

Cassie flashed a lascivious grin, grabbed the other clothes from Jen and headed off to the changing rooms.

**I knew you'd find good things. From the street I've watched you pick stuff out – everything you chose was just so predictable – sparkling, sleeveless, low-cut, bright – and most things Jen suggested were just ugly. She has no idea. She doesn't really have your best interests at heart, at least not like I do. There's something sublime about the way that dress feels when you let the silk run over your skin – it's so fine you almost don't feel it, can't register the sensation unless sight confirms it. I've felt the slippery cool of that dress and it feels good that if you buy it, I will have touched every inch that will touch you.**

Cassie sailed past the assistant, waving aside all offers to be escorted to a cubicle, heading straight for the back of the changing rooms where she dived into the furthest vacant one she could find.

She dropped everything on the floor and sank down onto the small stool, clasping both hands over her mouth. For five minutes she'd only been able to pant, somehow unable to draw a complete breath. Now she desperately tried to control the noise threatening to escape her. The panic attacks which had plagued her so regularly in her teens had stopped for a while, but seemed to have returned with a vengeance recently. She choked back the bile which burned her throat. Salt stung her eyes and angrily she brushed the tears away with the back of her hand. She wished she'd kept the little paper bag in her pocket but it had been so worn she'd thrown it away and forgotten to replace it. Instead, she hung her head forwards, letting her face go slack and after a few seconds, a little drool slid past her lips, dropping softly to the grey carpet tiles at her feet. She could feel the contracted muscles in her throat relax. Within a minute her breathing had returned to normal, the cramps in her throat receded and she sat back, letting quiet tears fall.

**When you ran off to the fitting rooms I waited, standing so still, just listening to my heart beat. It was**

**like you were dressing just for me. What took you so long?**

Jen had to admit, grudgingly, when Cassie emerged triumphant that it really was stunning despite having looked on the hanger as if it had been rescued at the last minute from a shredder. Now it looked fabulous. Scarlet, slinky, knee-length and strappy across the back, it seemed to coil around Cassie like a silk constrictor and be redefining gravity in quite spectacular ways.

'What do you reckon?'

**Perfect.**

'I hate you.'

Cassie beamed at her as she turned to see her profile in the mirror. 'It's not bad, is it?'

'Oh that's just beautiful on you! Are you going somewhere special?'

Cassie looked at the assistant. 'God, I hope so!'

**I drank in the vision of your reflection as you stared at yourself, almost unwillingly beautiful. I saw you turn your head to the assistant, but from where I stood I couldn't hear what she said. What could she have said? You looked stunning and in that moment I wanted you so badly I didn't know if I could wait.**

Jen giggled. 'How can you make such a silly thing look so good? What are you going to wear with it?'

215

'The biggest control knickers I can find, I think,' said Cassie, finally exhaling.

Jen's laughter followed Cassie as she went to change into the next outfit.

I didn't stay. I'd seen enough. I wanted time alone to think about you. All my planning stages were going so well and I was excited but still cautious…I've been hurt too often before.

Something special has to be done first to make you perfect.

# Chapter Nineteen

Too nervous to do any work, the morning of Cassie's date was spent loading the back of her mom's car with her office's unwanted Christmas presents. A quick drive across a quiet city meant she arrived at the local shelter during lunch and so there were plenty of volunteers to help unload. Having left her hat, scarf and gloves in the trunk, they were now buried beneath the mountain of donations so she was forced to supervise proceedings in between going for a stomp around the car to try and keep warm. She couldn't help but pour scorn on the mountain of ugly nonsense that was paraded before her. Cassie envisioned streets full of homeless guys in flashing-nose Rudolph jerseys all playing with an assortment of lumpen animals that went into spasm when you clapped or shouted. It was gonna be a weird old year.

Cassie was being watched from the shelter's doorway.

**Getting to see you twice in one week is a message I don't intend to ignore.**

Cassie made it home by a little after two in the afternoon as a feeble sun gave up the ghost, allowing the January chill to descend, the freezing cold nearly making her grind her teeth into dust.

Once safely indoors she cracked open a bottle of red and started to run a bath. Cassie was the mistress of being ready five hours early or an hour late. Take your pick. As the bathroom filled with steam she laid out the dress and tortuous underwear on the bed, cleared some of the accumulated plates and mugs from her desk and threw three days' worth of unopened mail into the recycling box by the door.

By the time her aging boiler had filled an entire bath, Cassie was pouring the last glass from the first bottle. She decamped to the bathroom.

**Bath time.**

She set the wine glass down on the little wooden stool by the taps, shrugged out her clothes and clambered into the ancient tub, sinking through cool bubbles into scalding heaven beneath. Sliding beneath the water, she let the heat wash over her, then sat up spitting bubbles and smoothed wet hair back from her face.

She lay back, reached for wine and drank deep. Rinsing the glass in the bathwater she toyed with it as she made herself some promises aloud.

'I will not get utterly mashed and disgrace myself. Or him.

'I will not wake up in his bed tomorrow.

'I will not go home with my knickers in my handbag,' although as she said this she pictured the suck-it-all-in nightmares and figured that without a crowbar, she didn't have much to worry about.

She dozed in the bath, letting ludicrous daydream after daydream filter through her deluded mind. There was the one where he stood by adoringly as she opened her first major exhibition in New York; the one where he sat in the audience looking on adoringly as she accepted her first Oscar; the one where he was grateful and adoring as she felled a violent street gang with her extraordinary martial arts skills. And then, for reasons she could never figure, the one where she was sobbing by his deathbed, finding all the right words to say, making a perfect daytime-movie widow. Every time stuff like this appeared in her imagination she'd find herself shedding real tears, as she did now.

'Ludicrous,' she muttered, hauling herself out the bath and leaving a trail of wet soapy footprints all over her apartment until she returned with a second bottle and the corkscrew. Back in the bath she rinsed her glass under the cold tap and got stuck in.

While Cassie was gathering enough Dutch Courage for a small country, Paul and Mac had gone off to shoot pool. As they were heading out, Paul had claimed not to be nervous about the evening, but all the time he was talking he was putting his shoes on the wrong feet.

'Pants on fire,' laughed Jen as she disappeared through to her study, relishing the time and opportunity to get some work done at home, but still she had her cell phone nearby, knowing full well that her afternoon was at the mercy of Cassie's pre-date panic. Except it didn't come.

By the time Cassie lurched out her bath she had enough red wine in her to feel invincible, sexy and afraid of nothing or no man. With Goldfrapp blaring from the stereo, she dried herself off in the bedroom and then stood defiant, naked and with hands on hips, staring at the control knickers.

'Right, you little bastards,' she growled, 'let's see what you've got.'

It started off well. Sort of. Just holding them up at eye-level, she tried stretching them as wide as they would go but even then they still looked no bigger than a glove. She turned them over, looking for the zipper that might make things a bit easier, but no such luck.

'Fine,' she muttered, bending over to step into them. Getting them past her calves to her knees was no problem and she was feeling rather optimistic. She had a very nice vision in her head (just like the air-brushed image on the packet) of being smoothed out in every conceivable direction, and making the dress look like it only had one woman inside it.

Two inches past her knees the knickers went on strike.

'Oh, come on!'

Cassie looked in the full-length mirror, saw herself bent double, her ass in the air and a pair of impossibly tight control knickers making her knock-kneed. Giggles started to wash through her and she had to make a real effort not to pee. She let the underwear fall to the floor and stood up to appraise her body properly.

She let out a long sigh. A season of comfort-eating seemed to have done more damage than she had been willing to admit. Tall and naturally slender, her belly, hips and thighs had all gone a bit doughy since she last checked.

'Shit.'

Then inspiration struck. She lay down on the floor – if it worked with jeans, it would work now.

After a furious twenty-minute struggle that was part howls of drunken laughter and stinging tears of frustration, she was sweaty and furious. Intoxicated and breathless, she panted like a puppy in summer till she could stand without being dizzy and stared at herself in the mirror, holding up the packet for a comparison.

'Lying bastards.' She glared down at them. 'You're coming off with a pair of scissors.'

She had to admit, though, that with the dress on, they did their job. Cassie made a mental note not to sit down or stand up too quickly for the rest of the night. Or cough, sneeze, hiccup, fart or eat anything.

She was ready by half-past-five. For an eight o'clock dinner. She took the dress off and sat down on the rug to rummage under the bed for shoes. Bending over the waistband of the knickers made her pant like a dog all over again.

I heard you moving about the bedroom and then the wall vibrated as you fell back against it. I pushed myself against the cold plaster, imagining I could feel a little of your warmth seeping through to touch me. I held my breath for a few moments, straining to hear yours. In that moment I wanted to confess everything, to prepare you for the trials ahead but that's only because I wanted you to know how much I cared, how much I was willing to do for us. Instead, I turned my face to the wall and tenderly kissed the bit where you were sitting, only an inch from me. I know it seems foolish but I whispered to the wall, 'Soon. We'll be together soon.'

Cassie found two matching heels and blew the dust off the black suede. Grabbing the headboard she levered herself to her feet then paced for half an hour, picking bits of yummy leftovers out the kitchen each time she went past. She swore to herself it was just to test the elasticity of her knickers. On her third pass she stopped with a chicken drumstick halfway to her mouth and looked down at her miracle underwear. She shrugged. 'In for a penny, in for three pounds…'

'I hate first dates.'

'Me too,' Cassie grinned at him as a waiter cleared away their starter plates.

She couldn't believe how smug she felt. An entire entrée without a single faux pas. She hadn't said anything too dumb or fallen over anything or had a random twitch and thrown red wine over anyone. This was going so well.

Paul refilled her wine glass. 'So come on, tell me your worst. S'only fair…I told you mine.'

Cassie stared at him. 'You're serious? Oh god there's so many!' Too late. Whatever bit of her brain was supposed to be guarding the entrance to her mouth had clearly snuck off to a bar.

'Oh hell, you really wanna know how bad it can be? You asked for it. One time…' and she launched into a catalogue of disaster that she figured should scare him more than enough.

'...so when I called that guy the next day, he couldn't stop laughing and he actually said, "Don't worry I'm not laughing at you", which brought histrionics from him and his workmates in the background. Then one time I heard the guy I was in bed with – who thought I was asleep – sneak through to his room-mates in the living room and ask them to break the "comedy" emergency condom picture they had on their wall as we'd run out of protection; and then another time my period started in the middle of a first date so I had to get home in a hurry, but as he said goodnight to me there was blood all over the back of my pants, which he didn't notice, but it meant I had to keep turning around so that he was never behind me, and I did a real lousy job of pushing him out the door without acting completely disinterested.'

Cassie got to the period story as two rare steaks were delivered to the table. Her diatribe came to a sharp halt. If her underwear had allowed, she would have curled up into a little ball.

'Just think,' she said, raising her eyebrows as their waiter left, 'now you have a new worst first-date story. I don't know about the Gents in this place but the Ladies has a window you could probably fit through.'

Paul's badly suppressed laughter suggested he wasn't going anywhere. He raised his glass to toast her.

'Here's hoping your disasters end here,' he said, never once breaking eye contact.

Cassie reached across to clink her glass against his but as she did, she was horrified to feel a bit of her dress gently ping and come undone somewhere behind her.

She concentrated on ploughing into the food in front of her, the steak having arrived with a side of sweet-smelling cous-cous chopped through with handfuls of fresh herbs. Desperate to escape to the bathroom and investigate her dress she was too afraid that, if she stood up, it would now unravel around her ankles and reveal her suction knickers. Not only that, but after just one mouthful she could feel a shrubbery's worth of greenery clinging to her teeth and so spent the entire main course bobbing her head up and down at everything Paul said, surreptitiously sucking her teeth whenever he blinked and always talking into her hand or napkin, trapped in her chair, praying the dress would stay put.

The rest of the meal went without incident and a quick check in her little mirror when Paul went to the bathroom reassured her that she didn't have green piano-key teeth. The dress was another problem. When she did finally stand, she did it clutching herself in ways she knew couldn't look good.

He had the restaurant call a cab and he took her

home. On her doorstep he told her what a fine time he'd had, what great company she was and how much he'd like to see her again. He kissed her lips oh-so-gently and got back in the cab. After the tail-lights disappeared, Cassie stood outside for a little while, oblivious to the cold, relishing the kind of date she'd always assumed normal, grown-up women had.

# Chapter Twenty

Of course, eventually even Nell was a disappointment.

For months after we broke up, I would still wake some nights at 4 a.m. and almost always because I had these crazy dreams about her. Usually she was standing on a raised stone jetty with her back to me, but I knew it was Nell because I could see where I scalped her. The jetty extended a half mile out over a beach with sand the colour of hot chocolate; the sea miles away in every direction. I had to get to Nell, only the sloping edges of the jetty were covered in bound bundles of what looked like sun-bleached twigs but really they were bones; hollowed femora and tibiae, the ends cut diagonally to make lethal spears that jutted in all directions. When I started to climb I saw Emily and heard her choking; saw Rachel on her knees, convulsing. I wanted more than anything for them all to look at me but they wouldn't.

I would hear the vibration before I felt it, a dull roar that seemed to come from inside me. I turned to see the tide coming in, only it didn't come in waves, it rushed over the sand, so fast it was unnatural – like it was on speeded-up film. In a panic I started to scramble over the bundles but slipped and threw a hand out to steady myself. I felt the soft inside of my wrist get skewered by a bunch of pointed bones. The water continued to rise at an unfeasible rate so I scrabbled faster, clawing my way over the spikes until I fell exhausted onto the cool slimy stone of the jetty. Nell looked down at me then, only to turn and walk away.

That's when I woke to find I was massaging my wrist and when I turned it over, I was sure that I would see five small perfectly round wounds. There was nothing.

I had the dream again a couple of weeks ago, only then I woke up in a different state. I suddenly realised all alone in the dark that I've been doing this wrong. I felt sick – just how stupid have I been? What a waste of years of my life. When I think about all the effort I put into it, all the thinking, the planning, the execution. I don't even remember why I thought it would work.

I mean, these women should never have let me down and I can't just be expected to forgive them; they brought it on themselves.

I know in my heart now that it was a mistake to think I could replace someone so easily. I'm not going to do it again. I won't, I mean I know it's wrong.

I guess you can't just replace a soul-mate.

See, all that pain I endured when Shauna was gone – well, obviously I can't replace her. She was unique.

But here's the thought that's finally hit me...if I can find a woman who's been through what I've been through, then that means we'll be totally perfect for each other. It's so simple. It'll be like finally finding my other half. She'll be my mirror image.

And if I can't find that woman, no matter. I can create one.

# Chapter Twenty-One

The next afternoon, flowers were delivered to Cassie's apartment. As she opened the door and saw the bouquet she assumed one of her neighbour's must be out. The delivery boy looked at her.

'Miss McCullen?' Cassie nodded and accepted the bouquet. She let the door swing closed behind her and drifted through to her kitchen. Rooting around for a vase, she read the note.

'Seeing as how your dress behaved itself, shall we try for a disastrous second date instead? Pick a terrible movie next Saturday. Pizza's on me afterwards. Paul x.'

It was too much. Freaking out, Cassie immediately sent him an SMS message explaining she would be out of town on business for a couple of weeks, thanked him for the flowers and said she'd see him soon. Relief washed through her. Then guilt. She went to fret in the shower.

The trip, at least, was genuine. Although she would rather have stuck pins in her own eyes than admitted she was afraid to fly, even her best avoidance tactics had crumbled in the face of an offer she couldn't resist. She was leaving the next week for an all-expenses paid and salaried two-week placement with a minor but respected agency in New York.

The morning of her departure she was washing her hair for the third time, telling herself that there was nothing to fear from planes, but it didn't work. She was just gonna have to get a little drunk.

By lunchtime she was hunched into a window seat, grinding her teeth together and picking the skin around her nails to pieces to get her through take-off. By the time they reached their cruising altitude she had made a long list in her head of all the different things that could happen to a plane that would involve it falling out the sky and plummeting her to an untimely and messy death. She'd just got to considering how such heavy engines stayed stuck to the underside of the wings when she caught a snippet of the conversation going on around her.

The couple next to her were trying to do the crossword.

'OK, Billy somebody, four letters, wrote "Uptown Girl".' Cassie saw the newspaper spread on his tray table and stared at him as he tapped his pen on the edge. She couldn't believe he could be so dim.

His girlfriend looked up from her bag of chips. 'Elliot?'

'No, four letters...'

At that point, someone chipped in from behind. Cassie twitched. She was surrounded.

The voice over her shoulder said, 'Wasn't that Mike and the Mechanics?'

She snorted back a laugh and stared fixedly out the window for five minutes while the couple and at least two of their friends in the row behind ran through a succession of defunct bands, entirely failing to get even close to the right answer.

When Cassie couldn't take it any more she turned to face her neighbours. 'Joel,' she growled at the guy on the end. 'J. O. E. L.'

She turned back to the window.

He seemed genuinely grateful. 'Thanks. OK, next clue...where was Hamlet set?'

His girlfriend thought she knew this one. 'Scotland?'

'No, that was Macbeth.'

'Wasn't he the Prince of Denmark?' said a voice from behind.

'Oh yeah,' shrieked the girlfriend. 'Oh! Norway! It's Norway.'

'Norway?'

'Yeah, Norway. How many letters?'

'Seven.'

'See? Norway! N.O.R.W.A.Y'

'Ok…N. O. R. W…oh, it doesn't fit…'

Cassie, in a moment of clarity and calm, started thinking that the engines failing and the plane being dashed to the ground might not be such a bad thing after all. She pushed her call button and ordered another drink.

Her return trip meant getting up around 4 a.m. for a 7 a.m. flight. By the time she touched down she was having trouble staying upright and felt that, pretty soon, one of these huge yawns was going to dislocate her face. She checked her phone only to find out that Jen couldn't come pick her up after all and she was going to have to get a cab. That didn't do much for her mood although she was dimly aware that the reason she was so angry was because after two weeks there was still no message from Paul.

The minor demons must have been asleep, though, because there was no queue at the full rank so within the hour she was home and asleep fully clothed, snoring like heavy furniture being scraped over a tiled floor.

That evening Jen came round with a bottle of red by way of apology.

Cassie opened the door with hair that was still

wet from the shower.

'How you doing, honey?'

'I'm vertical, my eyes are open, I'm scrubbed clean and I ate a banana. Do I get a prize?'

Jen held up the bottle.

'Hurrah! I win. Get in here, will ya?'

Jen apologised again for being dragged into a pointless meeting and not providing chauffeur duties as promised. Cassie shrugged it off.

'Hell, it was fine, I got a cab no problem. Only thing is, I asked him to let me sleep, and he laughed and told me lots and lots of stories about sleeping.'

The wine open, the girls were curled up at either end of Cassie's sagging, comfy red sofa and Jen had heard story after story about the placement. She was floored that Cassie could fit so much into a fortnight that should have been about work, work and more work.

'My B&B was a nightmare,' Cassie was moaning, 'just the maddest couple you can imagine. They both collect these giant fake porcelain dolls dressed in US State costumes and I swear there are around fifty of them in the house. The guy told me they like to move them around when the guests are sleeping to freak them out and make them think the house is haunted, or the dolls are possessed, or something. I was so weirded out. And they chose to open accommodation halfway up a block that has two of the most insanely dangerous drug-dealing corners I've ever had to walk past. I spent a fortune in cabs after these two whores grabbed my arm one morning and tried to get me to resolve an argument they were having about a realistic amount to charge for a handjob. Jesus, Jen, I swear. I mean, what are you supposed to say?' Cassie laughed. 'I just told 'em I thought they were selling themselves short charging just five bucks! As if that wasn't bad enough, I'd get woken every morning by the old couple in the next room slamming their bedroom door about 5 a.m. as they pounded across the landing to the bathroom to do god-knows-what. It sounded like they were coughing up the house cat. Bastards.'

Jen just stared. She wasn't sure if she was envious of Cassie's adventures, or thoroughly relieved that she got to spend her days with creatures that, at worst, blew bubbles at her.

'The best bit,' Cassie said, 'was that on our last night we got dragged to a 3D porn movie. Isn't that just hilarious?'

Jen wasn't sure about hilarious. Her entire experience of 3D had been a short piece of film about dead chickens falling off the end of a conveyor belt. Up until now, it wouldn't have occurred to her to make any erotic associations. Her imagination didn't get time to kick in. Cassie was in full flow.

'I really thought it would be so cool, you know? Except it was soft-core.' Jen was floored by how disappointed Cassie sounded, but kept her mouth shut. 'I mean, it's bad enough getting gunked in the eye for real, but to have it flying out the screen at you? Ohmigawd.'

Jen choked back her laugh so hard she got hiccups.

'As it turns out, the porn bits of the movie are not 3D. Weird things like the salt and pepper pots are 3D. The rest of it is full of dull close-ups of the untanned butts of many Sixties chicks in seriously huge panties, so there are massive gussets everywhere and it is the least erotic thing that has ever been paraded before my eyes. Totally bizarre. I only found out after that the movie was made in '69.' Cassie shook her head in mock disbelief and poured herself some more wine. 'Oh, and I've decided I'm gonna take up Tai Chi. I saw these guys doing it in this little basketball court every morning on my way to work, and it looks so cool.'

'What?' said Jen. 'Are you serious? I thought you always said you were gonna study a seriously violent martial art you could use for self-defence!'

Cassie looked hurt. 'This will be useful! If I'm ever attacked I will remember all my training and open a can of hummus on their ass.'

Their second date was even less disastrous. They rented Monty Python's *Life of Brian*, called out for pizza and got very drunk. The evening ended with them both slumped on the floor, stuffed full of take-out and singing *Always Look on the Bright Side of Life*. Cassie had forgotten to worry what he thought of her, even though she was quite used to people at concerts asking her to stop singing along as she was ruining their evening. On her turf, in jeans and a clean shirt, she just didn't care.

When Paul asked if he could stay over, she got up to lead him to the bedroom only to look behind her and see him clearing stuff off the sofa. She opened her mouth to say something but thought better of it. When she'd dug out enough blankets and sheets to make up a bed, he hugged her, told her what a fun night he'd had, kissed her lightly and wished her sweet dreams. Cassie was beginning to think he didn't fancy her at all.

She woke late, to the smell of bacon frying. Padding through to the kitchen, she found him whisking eggs for scrambling. She patted her fright-wig morning hair and set about making coffee. She was confused. The word for how she was feeling wouldn't come to her.

As they sat down to some *Simpsons* reruns with toasted muffins, bacon and scrambled eggs, fresh coffee and yet more bad jokes left over from the night before, Cassie finally got the word. Nice. This was nice.

By their fourth date, Paul was spending some work nights and almost every weekend at Cassie's. He figured if something was this effortless, it was worth diving straight in. Cassie, convinced that she had about another three months before Paul's delusional state wore off and he finally realised what a terrible mistake he'd made, enjoyed it for what it was. She truly believed that she didn't deserve this, didn't deserve something good. Every time he did something nice for her she felt worse. Couldn't he see her for what she was? Soon Paul would be with someone worthy of him and she would have been his one allowed bizarre, unstable transgression.

While Cassie was settling comfortably into her usual 'what's the worst that can happen?' outlook, Paul's company in London were able to arrange an extension to his visa. He'd also taken the liberty of talking to his boss about a secondment mooted too long ago to remember, putting in the long-distance call and filling his superior in on his recent progress, gradually leading up to real reason for getting in touch. He didn't get that far.

'Come on, what's her name?'

Paul grinned. 'Cassie. Cassandra if you really want to piss her off.'

'Do you really want to piss her off?'

'Jesus, no. She'd probably rip my nuts off.'

'So you want to stay out there? For a girl?'

'Uh-huh.'

'Are we ever going to see you back here? No pressure, obviously. I'm only asking because it would be good to take you out of the Lottery syndicate – would give us an extra grand each when we hit the jackpot.'

Paul suddenly missed his office very much. The feeling was powerful enough to make him feel momentarily nostalgic about the hour-long commute each way, the filthy air, the over-crowded streets, the lousy drinking hours…

'I don't know. But can we talk about it again in six months?'

'I suppose. You know, I used to admire your confirmed bachelorhood Paul. It was a real comfort to me. I take this personally.'

'Don't worry – chances are she'll give it a month then leave me for someone half my IQ but twice my income.'

'So there's hope for me yet?'

Five minutes of catching up on office gossip and the call was over. Paul had already decided he wouldn't tell Cassie that he'd engineered his stay there. As much as he hated to lie to her, he knew she would bolt if she knew he was this sure about them.

# Chapter Twenty-Two

By the end of that year, Mac had started helping Paul with the immigration process, and Paul's office in London had arranged things so he could stay in three month bursts and didn't need to spend more than a week out the country at any time.

**Cassie has a bath most nights about 8 p.m. If there's no music or TV on, I can hear the water running, sometimes a cork being wrenched from a bottle, sometimes snatches of a conversation. If one of them is on the phone, I hear everything.**

Cassie didn't miss having her own space, but she did miss being able to drink, freak out, cry, yell and behave like a spoilt brat. Now she had an audience. Someone normal. Which meant she had to behave, and that was a strain.

Even worse, she knew she thought she was falling in love with him and whatever malevolent spirits made up her dark streak continually urged her to just run and keep running. Jen kept telling her that this was all natural, for Cassie, and that she would settle into the idea that she'd found a good man and deserved to be happy.

Cassie nodded through these monologues, missing the anger that used to fuel her. As it had dissipated, so had her fire. She felt neutered. She wasn't special any more. Now she was just like everyone else.

Just like Jen.

Even with this sheet beneath me I still feel the chill of the cold concrete and the damp of the wall. I have an almost constant sniffle and have to muffle every cough and sneeze. Every time footsteps approach the door I scuttle across the floor to my hide. No-one has ever stopped at what I have come to think of as my door.

For a month I watched the building from the little park across the street and now know that Paul leaves early and works late, four days a week. Fridays he is home by mid-afternoon. He and Cassie have sex then. I always hear them. After that they go shopping for weekend food and lots of wine. Sometimes I let myself in to their apartment and lay in the sheets where they have lain. Sometimes I follow them out to the store and watch them shop.

Mostly I wait.

One foul winter evening Cassie was working late

on a series of shots that were driving her crazy. She was expected to work a miracle with the fourth-generation logo of a wacky bird that accompanied the cheesy font chosen by the client – Cheap Jeeps! – a peddler of rattly cut'n'shunt 4x4s run by an oily sleaze called Randall. Trying to pretty-up his staff – freak-show rejects all – was beginning to feel impossible. Pausing only to angrily slosh more wine into her glass, she hoped the regular designer's flu turned into scurvy to punish her for landing Cassie this thankless job. She hated this work. All she wanted was to get back to taking photos. The agency's senior photographer was on extended leave and unlikely to return. Cassie knew the job was almost hers and although her portfolio wasn't extensive enough to have properly earned the promotion, she knew that with just a couple of good opportunities, proving her abilities would be no problem. She fumed and mumbled and Paul knew better than to disturb her. He was already exhausted just thinking about his early start and was sitting staring at his presentation wondering if and when any of it would finally sink into his brain, when he realised he'd left his notes at the university.

'Ah, crap.'

Cassie looked up from what she was doing. Her expression suggested that only one of them was entitled to be having a bad night, and it wasn't him. Her face softened when he smiled at her, and she raised one eyebrow, turning round in her chair to face him, tucking one foot under her other leg and reaching for her glass.

'Left my notes in Mac's office at the uni,' he said, and she reached behind her and pulled the curtain back to check the weather.

'It's snowing again. You can't go out in this. Can't you get them in the morning on the way to the airport?'

**Yeah, on the way to the airport…**

The thought of getting up even earlier than 5 a.m. didn't exactly appeal, but then neither did leaving the saggy, cosy comfort of his armchair, wrapping himself in endless layers and braving the sub-zero temperatures.

'S'pose,' he grinned, and felt brave enough to ask. 'So how's the…'

She cut him off by turning sharply away and glaring at the monitor. 'Don't even ask,' she growled. 'If these people were any uglier I'd have no option but just to PhotoShop a bag over their mutated heads.'

Paul laughed and came across the room, wrapped his arms around her shoulders and kissed the back of her head. She didn't respond. When he looked up all he could do was gawp at the screen. 'Ouch,' he said into her hair, 'those are some seriously ugly people…you just wouldn't buy a used car from them would you?' And then he ducked to avoid a reasonably vicious and well-aimed punch that only just fell short of his ribs.

He winked at her from a safe distance then went to make a call. Cassie sat silently, listening in. An old habit, but one she didn't know how to break.

'Mac? Hey, Paul. Yeah I know – I was just about to give in for the night… 5 a.m.'s gonna kill me.' There was silence for a few minutes, punctuated with a few 'yeahs' and an uproarious laugh, which just made Cassie smile.

'No, left my notes in your office, so why don't I pick you up in the morning and we can go via the uni and have breakfast somewhere on the way? It'll mean only paying parking for one car at the airport.' A pause. 'Shithead. I want ringside seats when karma comes to kick your smug ass. OK, see you at check-in at six, then. And you are so buying breakfast.'

Paul hung up and came back through. 'Mac wants the extra hour in bed, for which he's prepared to pay airport parking for four days. I hate him.' He yawned a huge, exaggerated, expansive yawn and stretched like a bear in Spring. He went to Cassie, leant down, held her chin lightly with one hand and kissed her goodnight. 'Don't work too late, angel.' He kissed her again, savouring the taste of warm red wine on her lips, then he headed to bed.

Alone in the dark of their bedroom, he set his cell phone alarm to vibrate, then slipped it under his pillow. He shucked out his clothes and climbed into Cassie's side of the bed to warm it for her before scooting over to his own side when it was no longer scary to stretch his feet right down to the end. He didn't hear her come to bed, but he sure as hell felt her freezing cold feet as she jammed them between his. He wriggled round and pulled her close.

When his pillow wobbled him awake at 4 a.m., he slid as gently from the bed as he could manage in the freezing pre-dawn but he needn't have bothered – Cassie snored like a faulty waste-disposal unit. He shivered his way into the bathroom, grateful for a hot shower that might just be enough to insulate him against their polar cap of a kitchen.

Half-an-hour later, and clutching a huge coffee, he felt as close to human as anyone rising at such an ungodly hour could possibly feel. He opened the tiny icebox and took the flower gently from its carton, then went back to the bedroom where Cassie had switched pitch and now sounded more like a wounded Chewbacca trying to be heard above an avalanche. He lay the orchid on his pillow and kissed his girl goodbye, brushing matted hair from her forehead.

Her breathing settled as he did so and she curled up into a ball. Right then, more than anything in the world, he wanted to slide right back into bed, curl up around her and hibernate through the rest of the Winter. Knowing that a mere knight's move away Mac was still in bed wrapped around a warm woman made Paul determined to save his appetite for the most expensive breakfast he could find.

Grabbing his bags and keys and a flask of boiling water for the car-lock, and donning gloves, scarf and a beanie, he opened their front door and crept along the hall and down one flight into the foyer where took a deep breath and opened the main door.

'Fucking hell,' he muttered, grinding his teeth together, making a swift mental note to himself never, ever under any circumstances to ever, ever, ever get up before the sun again as long as he lived. Winter sun wasn't up to much, but it was better than this. Toronto Winter was one of the few things that made him pine for the relative banality of London weather.

He made his way carefully down the icy steps, then crunched over fresh snow to the car. Lock warmed, he hopped in, amazed that it could be colder inside the car than out. His butt chilled the instant it came into contact with the icy leather. As he sat trembling, he cursed the forgetfulness that had cost him an extra hour in bed. Key in the ignition, the engine sounded about as happy as him to be woken this early but, whispering encouragement, prayer and thinly-veiled threats, he got both their chilled bones moving and headed towards the highway, switching lanes at the last minute as he remembered he needed to go via the university.

There were already footprints on the snowy road and Paul felt nothing but sympathy for the poor soul who had to be up even earlier than him.

On the drive over, Paul was willing to admit there was something exceptionally beautiful about the way the Winter world looked with no-one else in it. The slip of crescent moon looked like a careless rip in the velvet-blue sky and, with every tree dipped in deference towards the earth under the weight of new snow, he finally understood where Disney got it from. Stopped at a red light he figured two things. One, that if either of them could be dragged out of bed, he and Cassie should sneak out one morning and come build rude snowmen, then cover their tracks back to the house…and two, it was proof of minor demons that there were red lights at all at four in the damn morning.

It was Cassie's thing, the minor demons. She figured that on some forgotten layer of hell too low, sulphurous, foul and dank even for her worst clients, spare minor demons lay around scratching their sores, playing poker and being faxed lists of petty chores designed to increase the blood pressure of unsuspecting mortals, one point at a time. Just for the hell of it. She'd first mentioned this to Paul pretty early in their relationship when she was still making a real effort to scare him off. On waking one morning he'd made the mistake of asking her how she'd slept. She'd told him. 'Last night I dreamt I was awake. For eight hours I dreamt I was having real difficulty getting to sleep. I tried everything, but just couldn't drift away. And now I've woken up. I promise you, right now a spasm of minor demons are high-five-ing each other, the fetid little shits.'

Paul had just stared at her, not sure whether to laugh, run screaming for the hills or sympathise, and so she'd explained. She was convinced that everything from hitting every red light as you tried to catch a flight, but every green one on the way to a smear, was proof enough. Or when you made your favourite sandwich with the last of the ingredients in the fridge, and just before you took a huge bite, you saw a teeny patch of blue mould on the bread. Or when you came home and changed into your PJs and poured yourself a vodka then realised there were no mixers left and you had to get dressed and go back out again. In the pissing rain. Or when you got to the supermarket and waited half a lifetime in the queue, only to

remember you'd left your plastic in your other jeans.
Or when you taped the last episode of your favourite
show, but forgot to set it to the right channel and got
an hour of some Jessica Fletcher 'special' by mistake.
Or when you realised halfway through a meeting that
you've got your thong on sideways and that's why it
feels like you're garrotting yourself. She'd paused for
breath, grinned and said, 'OK, maybe I have to take
the blame for that one, but all the rest...' then she
caught herself in the mirror and said, 'And now I look
like nine kinds of shit. If you want to leave me, now's
probably a good time – I think this is as good as I
get.'

Paul grinned all alone in the car as he remembered how late they'd run into respective offices that
morning, both grinning like idiots and him with half
his clothes on inside out.

He had to concentrate on his driving. Thinking
of Cassie naked would only make him turn the car
round and blow off this entire trip. He tried to think
himself through his presentation, but his mind kept
wandering and he found himself debating whether
the stage would have a lectern, and how big it would
be, and if Cassie could hide inside and...this wasn't
helping at all. He turned the radio on and found
himself the victim of Celine Dion in full warble. No
more thoughts about sex, there you go, simple as that.

He'd been aurally castrated.

The university car-park was deserted apart from two rust-buckets he guessed were the cleaners' and he applied the brakes somewhere near the front of the building, abandoning his own heap after it slid across an icy patch to a creaking halt at a ridiculous angle across at least two spaces.

There were a few lights on the ground floor and one near the door, so at least the janitor would be around to let him in. He geared himself up for the blast of cold air as he opened the door.

It was snowing again and all he wanted to do was get in and out as quickly as possible, then go make Mac buy him a construction breakfast that would floor a weightlifter in training.

Construction breakfasts were one thing that Paul knew, long before he met Cassie, would never really let him leave Canada, even if he'd wanted to. The first one he'd had still ranked as a quasi-religious experience. Before coming to Toronto he'd taken a brief detour up the coast to Montreal where some guys in a bar had invited him to a house party. He didn't know where it was – he'd been way too drunk when he arrived – but it was in a gorgeous walk-up in a cute part of town. The doors and windows had been opened in an effort to combat the Summer humidity but it hadn't made much difference. There were fans running in each of the rooms – a front room cleared for space to dance, with low, soft chairs and cushions in a pile at the other end by the open windows.

To get to the kitchen you walked through a den which held the TV, some sculpture and two glass cases each housing some beautiful reptile. Paul had been embarrassed to discover he'd been trying to feed a Dorito to a scaly rock for nearly an hour before he spotted the actual lizard lurking in a corner, glaring at him with what he'd drunkenly decided was contempt. The hostess's house speciality, in hand when he arrived, was several racks of twelve-inch-long test tubes, three-quarters filled with vodka and topped with cranberry. The last thing he remembered of that night, after slugging some whisky and throwing up in the back garden, was accepting a fifth shooter, then nothing. Although he suspected he may have danced. The memory always makes him cringe. And probably everyone else too. He knows he dances like a puppet with its strings all knotted. Still, the next morning he'd woken curled up on the sofa, covered by a blanket and being regarded by a curious tabby, which was a gentle enough way to greet the mother of all hangovers.

He'd been invited to Cora's for a survivor's construction breakfast, which is where he'd been converted. Honestly, if his plate had arrived heralded by harp-clutching cherubs and a shaft of brilliant heavenly light he wouldn't have been in the least surprised. Less plate, more platter: you could barely see the pattern for the six slices of crispy bacon, four fried eggs, four sausages, a heap of mouth-watering home fries, hash browns, mushrooms, tomato and beans. He had never figured out why there was fruit on the side, but he ate that too. Then the basket of toast arrived. Then the coffee. Then the orange juice. Then the basket of warm bagels. Then the bowl of full-fat cream cheese.

Paul had nearly proposed to his waitress.

Thinking about it now was making him drool. He got out of the car and headed towards the main steps beyond the small bank of trees at the car-park's perimeter.

Mac had set his alarm for the same time as Paul, but had no intention of getting out of bed. Jen had mumbled something unintelligible and turned over when Mac moved, but he just lay in the dark and watched her sleep. He loved how quiet the world could be while all the birds were congregating on lawns, learning the day's new dance steps. Sneaky creatures. If he'd been at his parents place he would have swum in the lake and then indulged in an extended sauna, but here he just loved to wake Jen up properly, which in his book meant her screaming the neighbours awake and them both getting to work an hour late. He'd had no complaints so far. He lay in quiet contemplation of just what he was about to do, until he'd teased himself enough and with a filthy grin, he moved under the covers like a whale gliding below the ocean surface.

# Chapter Twenty-Three

Cassie had been running late, as always, and trying to do five things at once wasn't helping. She knew Paul would call when he landed and she felt in her handbag to make sure she had her cell with her.

The fresh orchid now clipped into her hair was always left on the pillow when he was going away as his idea of a quiet goodbye kiss. She'd seen it in the icebox the night before when she'd sneaked a spoonful of Ben & Jerry's, but hadn't said anything. Looking down she realised she had odd boots on.

'Crap, crap, crap,' she muttered, clattering down onto the hall floor and pulling them both off, undecided as to which pair to settle on. She was supposed to have this contact sheet at her designer's across town in twenty minutes and didn't have a hope in hell of making it.

'Black boots. No, brown boots. No, black boots.' She held one of each up to the light at arm's length, then held one against each thigh, comparing them with her red skirt. 'Black, definitely.' But as she pulled the first one on, she changed her mind.

'I'm so dead, so dead, just so, so, so dead...'

Brown boots on, she skipped down the stairs, yanked the building door open and without looking outside, hooked one foot around the jamb to stop it closing just to have a quick final rummage in her bag, rifling through its dark recesses trying to match random objects with a mental checklist...

'...keys, gum, keys, cell, keys, diary, keys, cash, keys, candy....whatever.' The important thing was her keys. Just once, with Paul at conference, she'd like not to have to call Jen and admit she'd locked herself out. Again.

It wasn't that she worried about his flight, it was more about him being in a luxury hotel for three nights. There would be women in the hotel. Paul had never given her reason for one second to think that he realised other women even existed. She trusted him. Yes, she trusted him. In fact, if she said it often enough without pausing in between, she believed it. She knew, however, this wasn't about Paul, it was about her. Yes she loved him, that wasn't in question, even though the very idea scared the crap out of her, but what was in perpetual doubt was her slightly subjective concept of fidelity. She knew that if it was her away for a long weekend of drinking and double beds and fun bathrooms, she wasn't sure she'd come home with a clear conscience. She'd yet to test the theory and was just very slightly freaked out by the idea that she might have found someone to be faithful to. Just the thought of him made her smile. Her designer would wait.

Finally satisfied that yes, she did have her keys, she tried to leave the building but found her way blocked by two men. Blinking into the morning Winter sun, she'd smiled at the older of the two, nodded down at her feet and said, 'I should have worn the black ones, right?'

# Chapter Twenty-Four

Paul had woken on cold ground, at first only aware of a dense pounding across the back of his head. He lay for a moment, willing the waves of nausea to settle and trying to lock down the last clear thing he remembered, anything to help him understand why he was now laid out on the freezing ground. He tried to look down at himself and would have screamed at the agony such a small movement induced, but pain shot through him from so many different points he thought he would faint.

'I wouldn't try to move,' said a man's voice.

Even though his senses were deadened by the intense pre-dawn cold, Paul realised he was close to completely numb. He didn't dare try to move again. His head was tipped so far back that all he could see was a hint of a storm-ready sky through the green-black of trees.

He urged his sluggish brain to think this through. He'd only been around the university properly a few times but knew that the only woodland was at the back of the administration buildings and it seemed unlikely that one man would have taken him far. The idea of why flared briefly but Paul slammed it down.

He could feel rough bark against the back of his head and could see no light from the nearest building, which meant they must be on the highway side of the woods, putting them at least a quarter of a mile from the car-park. Even if he could have screamed, Paul doubted anyone would have heard him. He tried to draw enough breath to speak, but searing pain shot through every muscle in his face and neck.

'I wouldn't try to speak, either.' Paul was reduced to panting short, sharp, sore breaths as he made an effort to control his rising panic.

Skirving finished tying Paul's hands together behind the tree, then came around to face him.

Paul tried to think back. He remembered just dumping the car and heading for the steps. He hadn't heard or seen anyone else.

Skirving stood over Paul, watching him intently, then pulled on a pair of latex gloves and reached into a plain blue rucksack hanging from a low, stumpy branch. He took out a small, pale, weekend leather case that Paul instantly recognised. It was his. He stared at the red wine stain spread across the front – he'd been in Schiphol airport, dozing on a bar stool when he'd woken just enough to hear his name being called for a last chance to board his flight. He'd leapt out of the chair, sending the wine flying all over his case and a pair of shoes he'd really liked, and run what felt like the length of Amsterdam to get to his gate.

Fear gripped Paul in the pit of his stomach and it was really only then that he realised fully just how bad things were, and how much worse they were likely to get. He tried to focus on the man's face – it seemed familiar but no more so than anyone you saw every morning on your commute. Who the hell was he? Then he got it. The case…The man had been at their door. That's where he knew him from. He felt a rush of goose-bumps wash over his freezing skin. Oh god, Cassie…

The man reached inside the case and pulled out Paul's old, worn-thin black and scarlet leather driving gloves. Suddenly aware of just how frightened and confused he felt, Paul tried to concentrate on what the man was saying.

'Don't think that seeing my face is going to be any help. I promise you, you're not going to live long enough to do anything about it.'

Paul felt warmth on his leg and became aware of a small cloud of noxious steam. He didn't think he'd ever wet himself before. The man tutted, reached out and ran his fingers through his victim's hair.

Paul squirmed and nearly fainted at the spasms of pain that wracked through his upper body. His only thought then was of a way to untie his hands and let the blood back to where he needed it, suddenly aware of how appallingly cold he was. He focused on this one target, determined he could find a way out of this. He wondered, briefly, if Mac had staged this prank, if he would step out from behind a nearby tree, laughing fit to burst, full of insincere apologies and photographs that would haunt Paul for ever. But then Skirving spoke again.

'Is Cassie still in bed, Paul? I like to know that she's warm and safe until I can be there to take care of her myself, see?'

Paul stared at him, all thoughts of Mac gone.

'Let's see if I can guess all the moronic questions you want to ask, Paul…first, why can't you speak? Am I right? I bet I am. This,' he crouched down, reached out and Paul felt the pressure as the man touched what was under his neck, 'is a Heretic's Fork. It was used to encourage the wayward to see the error of their ways, oh, a long time ago.'

The man giggled. 'So simple – it was never designed to kill anyone although it does seem a terrible waste of its potential to keep it for only external use.'

The man winked at Paul. 'But no, once someone recanted they were burned at the stake or hanged.

Nice traditional executions. They saved things like impalement for the perverts, I guess. I just love that quick deaths were never a priority for any of the Inquisitions. And this piece really is a work of art. Twelve inches of iron with four small spikes at each end, slightly opened like those crappy fairground claws you can never grab anything with. Well, the four at the top are buried in the soft tissue under your chin and the four at the other end will eventually splinter your sternum. But try speaking…you can't, can you? Genius. I had it made specially. As for breathing, you might want to remain calm.'

The man giggled again. Tears rolled silently down Paul's face.

'Just bear with me for five minutes, Paul, then we'll get on with the good stuff, OK?'

Skirving disappeared from Paul's line of sight and he could hear him as he moved around on the plastic sheeting. When he returned, he stretched, rubbed his hands together and stamped his feet. He leant back against a tree and addressed Paul.

'Jesus it's cold, isn't it? Anyway, why me, why am I here, how do I know Cassie, blah blah blah, right? I'll start at the beginning, shall I?'

Stepping forward until he was standing over him, Skirving started to speak but Paul was shocked to see his composure break almost immediately.

'I made…I lost…I…' The man turned away for a moment. When he turned back he seemed almost friendly.

'Do you ever watch those reconciliation shows, Paul? You know, the ones where they find a long-lost relative and reunite them with their family? Ever since I was a little kid I've loved those. Just loved them. I always got so emotional, even though they were total strangers to me! Crazy, huh?'

Paul currently had his own ideas on what constituted crazy but was in no position to share them.

'So the more I watched, the more addicted I got. I mean, I couldn't even go for a pee till I saw those people all hugging each other and crying and the host pretending to be all choked up, but really crying with happiness about their ratings, you know? Soul-less bastards. But it got me thinking how badly I wanted to feel something so intense. The idea of being so moved that I wouldn't mind crying in front of a snivelling audience, and millions of viewers. And I wanted to feel something that bad, I really did. But I don't even like the relatives I got at home, so why would I want to go digging up someone long-lost?'

Paul stared as the man stood perfectly still, lost in telling his story.

'In the end I didn't have to do a damn thing, though, Paul, because she came to me. Just like that.

Like it was the easiest thing in the world.'

Skirving let loose a blast of high, girlish giggle.

'When I think of all the time and energy I wasted…'

Skirving shook his head, gently laughing to himself. Then he crouched down and spoke to Paul quietly and deliberately.

'I lost the one thing that gave my life meaning, do you understand? And the idea that time would make that hurt less is bullshit. She was more real to me after she died.' Skirving hesitated, looking almost as if he might cry. 'I've never been able to let go of the idea of her. That's my world.'

While the man was speaking, Paul had tried in vain to work his bonds loose, but now Skirving smiled down at him and checked behind the tree. He steadied himself and placed one foot on Paul's chest, applying just enough pressure to cause Paul to pant heavily, his eyes wide with fear.

'Pay attention, Paul. Nearly finished now.' He took his foot from Paul and stamped it on the ground.

Skirving suddenly stopped talking and stared at Paul, but the only movement was a small shudder that ran through him. 'You should know, Paul, that if that weak bitch Nell hadn't failed me so badly I would never have had to move on and would never have found Cassie. So you should blame her and not me for what's about to happen. And Cassie won't fail me.' He paused and looked off into the woods. 'That would be bad.'

Skirving stepped forward and pushed Paul's head back a little, then pulled the iron spikes from his chin, carefully lifting the other end from his chest. Paul gasped and choked as he tried to draw in a full breath, revolted as he saw his own blood drip from the iron spikes. Before he could do anything, a bundle of cloth was balled into his mouth, a length of duct tape wrapped around his jaw to hold it in place. Then Skirving reached around the tree and cut the ropes holding Paul's arms. Paul fell sideways, his numb limbs no use to him. Skirving used the edge of his boots to nudge Paul over until he lay on his back in the centre of the huge piece of plastic sheeting draped all around the tree. He stood over him, one foot against each of his thighs and from a pocket took out a scalpel, holding it before Paul's eyes until his pupils widened in terrified recognition. It was such a small, light sliver of silver that it seemed ridiculous it could be considered a weapon, but the man's eyes left Paul in no doubt what his intentions were. Paul started to cry.

Skirving cocked his head to one side, watched for a few minutes, then he said, 'There's a bigger picture,

Paul, and I want you to try and see the world as it should be. The way I see it. I mean, yes, I'm going to hurt you. I could kill you straight away, but I've been very patient and it's been a while since I had any fun. You're the first guy I've ever been able to tell all this to, you know that? Like a bonding thing,' and he giggled again. 'So yes, you're going to be in excruciating pain, but only for the short time until you die. And after you die, it'll be me that makes Cassie's world whole because I finally realised I've been doing it wrong all along. That's kinda humiliating.

'I finally figured that she needs to go through what I've been through because then she'll understand me better than anyone else in the entire world. When she hears what's happened to you it'll be me who dries her tears and comforts her and heals her wounds. She'll come to love me for that, because she'll find me the only person who will truly understand her. Her life really is so shallow now – I mean, she really can be such a selfish, manipulative, childish bitch sometimes, can't she? Or did you think that part of her charm? She needs some perspective and only I can give it to her. I'm about to validate her life.'

Paul had lain very still as the man talked, wondering if there was anything he could do or reach or try that would buy him some time or give him the smallest chance, but his mind was sluggish with rapidly encroaching hypothermia and the man's constant talking was becoming hypnotic. He tried to send messages through his arms to his hands but his heavy flesh failed to respond and as he felt consciousness threaten to abandon him, he knew he was going to die without presenting even the slightest resistance.

'I'm so cold, are you? Let's get some heat going, shall we?' And with that Skirving dropped to his haunches, lay the scalpel aside and took a pair of scissors from his left pocket. He started to cut Paul's clothes away and within minutes Paul lay naked.

Skirving took the scalpel and swiftly pushed it into Paul just below the hip bone, then steadily drew it down the length of his leg, stopping just above his ankle. Paul screamed into the gag but the man calmly leant down and made a show of warming his hands in the steam where Paul's hot blood met freezing air.

As Paul's other leg was cut the same way, he screamed, and kept screaming, but didn't pass out. He willed himself to give in, to let the madman do what he wanted, but his stunned mind couldn't let go of the fact that this man knew Cassie. When she saw him, she might let him into their home without a second thought. Paul couldn't just roll over and die, couldn't leave her, he had to warn her, protect her. He had to tell himself he could take anything if it meant there was the smallest chance he would get to go home again.

As Paul's blood pumped thickly across the plastic, it pooled against the edge, a little spilling into the snow, staining it a vivid scarlet, his tormentor seemed entranced by the languid spread of crimson frost.

Skirving prepared to cut Paul again, then seemed to think better of it. For one glorious instant, as his captor stood up, Paul thought he might give up, let him go, just turn out to be mad and not really capable of going through with it all. But he was wrong.

The man stretched, rotated his neck to either side, then bent down close into Paul's face and said, 'I'm going to take your gag off cos it's in the way, but if you so much as draw breath to scream or shout for help, I'll jam this blade into your mouth so hard it'll impale your tongue to the back of your skull. Do you understand?' Paul nodded dumbly, and the gag was removed.

Choking for air, all Paul could say was Cassie's name over and over again, his mind flooded with images of her curled asleep, an orchid waiting for her so she'd know how much he adored her and hated to be away from her, even for four days. He wished he hadn't been asleep when she'd come to bed last night. He wished he'd told her he loved her. And all he could say, as he slowly bled out, his sluggish mind crippled with fear and cold, was a whisper, 'Baby I just want to come home. Cassie...,' and he cried, his tears barely on his skin before they froze.

'Adorable. Are you done? I'm bored.' And then Skirving cut both Paul's arms, slicing into the deltoid muscle at his shoulder and drawing the blade down as far as the backs of his hands. Then grabbing each wrist in turn he raised the bleeding limbs and cut Paul on a wide sweep from his armpits across his rib cage to the middle of his belly.

Paul was unconscious long before the blade was finally taken to his face, where his skin was slit from ear to ear, tracing a ruby line along his jawbone.

Skirving eventually stood and stretched again, careful not to get too near any of Paul's wounds. The cuts were symmetrical like anatomical illustrations and he felt real satisfaction at a job well done. But he was far from finished. He rubbed his gloved hands together. Damn, but it was cold. Then he took a small black leather case from his other coat pocket and opened it flat in the palm of his left hand. He placed the scalpel inside, then took three other items out, closed and replaced the case, knelt down on a smaller plastic groundsheet and set to work.

It had only been forty five minutes since Paul had first regained consciousness, and Skirving had heard three other cars arrive in the car-park. Staff were here and the sun would soon breach the horizon.

Finishing up, he stood, carefully bound his feet

in refuse sacks and secured them with tow rope tied around his calves.  Reaching above him he lifted his rucksack down, replaced the leather case, then used the smaller groundsheet a little at a time to cover the distance to the roadside, away from the car-park and all prying eyes. Once on the slushy tarmac he rolled it up and stuffed it into his bag, removed the refuse sacks and his shoes, replacing them with an ancient pair of donated, second-hand sneakers. Then he walked to the nearest bus stop, lightly dragging a fallen branch behind him to erase any tracks. At the shelter he waited, alone. He wanted to laugh. Cold, drained and with all the adrenaline of preparation and anticipation worn off, he knew his celebrations could wait. What he wanted most now was something warm to drink and to be as near to Cassie as possible. They would be coming to see her soon.

Joe Ramirez had been a caretaker at the university since his apprenticeship aged seventeen. In the forty-two years since then he reckoned there wasn't much he hadn't seen. Getting access to areas people didn't expect him to be was one of the perks of the job, wasn't it? People had a habit of abusing privileges, particularly with keys and a building they assumed was empty just because the lights were off.

Still, the best thing about being around students

– apart from watching them fucking the whole damn time – was the constant supply of excellent grass. Joe had a terrible habit of accidentally leaving certain doors unlocked in return for the best buds that rich kids parents' money could buy.

He'd nodded at his own apprentice, Billy, before sneaking out for his morning pick-me-up. There was a constant supply of the big fat joints that somehow regularly found their way into his locker. Billy had just grunted his acknowledgement and carried on having a serious rummage about his nose with his filthy index finger. Little short of the building burning down could have torn him away from his porn, and he sipped at his cooling coffee as he watched Joe step outside. He figured he was good for another half hour, and it would have been rude to leave Tammi just as they were getting acquainted.

Joe walked a little away from the building before lighting up. He wasn't really afraid of getting caught – after all, he had enough dirt on most of the staff to let him get away with murder – but there seemed no sense in inviting unnecessary headaches into his cushy world. He wandered among the trees, delighting in the early morning light filtering through the branches which cast a peachy glow on slivers of fresh powder snow. He took a long draw on the joint, savouring the breath before slowly exhaling. He wasn't really thinking about the path he took and so it took a moment for his slightly fuddled brain to process what was laid out on the ground before him. At first he thought wolves had torn a dog apart, but a second look and he knew it was too big to be any kind of domesticated animal. Besides, it didn't smell like any carcass he'd ever had to shift. He approached on shaking legs and retched when he saw what remained of Paul Docherty.

Backing away, he slipped and fell, scrabbling to get back to his feet by grabbing hold of a tree and pulling himself upright. A shower of powder snow covered him, ran down the inside of his collar, but it didn't register on skin already slathered in goose-bumps.

Then, despite the nausea rising in him, he turned back around and stared at the monstrosity spread out before him.

When Billy heard the scream, he dropped his battered copy of *Barely Legal*, leapt from the recliner and started towards the door, but the second scream stopped him in his tracks. If it was human, it sounded beyond any help that Billy could offer. He looked around what passed for their staff-room, wishing for once there were more crew on the early shift so he wouldn't have to go out there on his own.

He stood with his mouth open listening for more noise from outside, but the silence was worse than the preceding shrieks. Shaking his head and muttering about their shit union and not being paid enough for this crap, Billy took his coat and hat from the chair and unwillingly pulled them on as he made for the back door.

Once outside he hugged himself against the bitter cold and, mumbling curses to a god he almost believed in, wished a small portion of hell on whatever was dragging him away from fantasies of wicked Tammi and her need for a good spanking.

'Joe?' The only sound that answered him was one dollop of snow tumbling from an unseen laden branch.

'This isn't fucking funny, man.' Still nothing.

Billy started walking, but tried to keep within the glow of the service door he'd left wide open. He hadn't gone fifteen feet when the diffused light petered out. For comfort, Billy allowed his mind to wander and was so distracted with thoughts of all the wicked girls he knew in need of a sound spanking that he nearly fell over Joe who was crouched, face down in vomit-spattered snow, crying like a lost child.

'Jesus, man...' stuttered Billy, stumbling back. 'What the fuck...?'

And then, looking beyond Joe, what he saw made him scramble away from his boss, away from the dark of the woods, away from his nightmares made flesh and into their office where he kept his own breakfast down just long enough for his shaking hands to dial 911.

# Chapter Twenty-Five

I wish I'd brought a camera.

# Chapter Twenty-Six

'Man, I hate this bit. I hate it when they cry.'

'You'll show some fucking respect. The identification will be far worse than this. Wait till she sees what the sick fuck did to him. Come on.'

Cassie had assumed the two men on her doorstop were yet another passing cult come to swell their numbers and she had wondered, briefly, if seeking fashion advice from random religious fanatics was really the smartest thing she'd done that morning. She was about to skirt around them with a glib claim to be Jewish and beyond the reach of any conversion, but something about the men made her keep quiet. The way they dressed and their polite silence persuaded her they weren't religious.

'Miss McCullen?' asked the younger. Cassie nodded, dumbly. Something was very wrong, but she didn't want to think what.

The older man spoke next. 'I'm afraid I have some bad news for you. Can we go inside?'

Cassie doesn't remember much else. She was escorted up the one flight to her apartment and, once seated, heard the man tell her that a Markus Lindberg (she barely recognised the name – Mac had been just Mac for so long) had called the police when Paul failed to either turn up at the university, or the airport. He'd not been able to reach him on his or his girlfriend's mobile (that's when she remembered switching it to silent when she'd worked late the night before) and had missed the flight. This was unlike Paul. Mr Lindberg had been afraid that Paul might have had an accident driving in the early morning icy conditions. Cassie nodded throughout, waiting for them to get to the bad news. She stared at her brown boots, only noticing for the first time the frayed stitching and bald patch on the toe. She should have worn the black ones.

Mac's call had come within ten minutes of a 911 call from university staff. The police had found Paul's car, they said, abandoned in the campus car-park. They'd found his body not far away. A positive identification had been made. She heard him say something about dental records and wondered why they couldn't just look at his face. She made eye contact with the older man and asked to see Paul, but the men looked at each other; the younger one said nothing, just stared at the floor.

'We wouldn't advise it, Miss McCullen. There's… well, there's been substantial damage done to the body and we feel it would distress you unnecessarily to see it for yourself.'

Cassie wanted to know exactly what. She doesn't know why she had to do it, but she's lived long enough to regret seeing him one last time.

Just then there was a key in the door and her mom, Mac, Jen and her parents were there. Cassie recalls the oddest thing – it was at this point she thinks she went deaf, like after a swim when she couldn't shake all the water from her ears. And then all she could think was, 'Why did everyone know before her? Wasn't Paul hers?' She saw Mac was crying, which is when she remembered to cry, too. She doesn't think she's ever remembered to stop.

# PART THREE

# Chapter Twenty-Seven

This dream, like all the others, started out in what felt like real time, as if the last eighteen months had been some dreadful nightmare and everything was really OK. There he was, smiling at her. It was the thing she loved most about him, that he smiled. He smiled at her when she was being a pain, he smiled at rude people to make them go away. He smiled when she bitched about her day, and he smiled as he opened his eyes to her every morning.

Then the dream changed and she looked for him but he was gone. Instead she was on a beach bound on three sides by high brick walls. Along the back wall were some spectators, hundreds of feet above where Cassie and some others like her stood on dark sand. The waves never crashed on the ground, instead they approached the tiny stretch of beach and tall, tumultuous, livid, muscular dark waters scooped them all up and crashed them against the brick, always just out of reach of those at the top who tried in vain to rescue them. With each crash she felt her bones shatter like a cheap wine glass in hot water but somehow, deposited back on the sand she was whole again and waited calmly as the next wave approached.

She's had this dream so often that she is resigned to the violence and viciousness of it.

She wakes retching, as she often seems to. As her brain registers consciousness, her constricting throat sends panic through her, and she sits bolt upright in bed, gasping for breath, her ribcage heaving, dread shaking her inside and out.

The constrictions hurt and she chokes back sobs, reaching for the worn paper bag by the bed and uses it, like an asthma sufferer, to get her breathing back under control.

Her sleep is often shot through with frightening images and threatening dreams, but she accepts these as a part of her. She knows the mechanics of grief well enough and wishes, in her lucid moments, that her fractured subconscious would give her just a little bit of a break.

She no longer keeps a clock by her bed – it never matters what time it is – so instead Cassie reaches out and pulls the curtain back just enough to see the day, but it's hard to tell if it's the glass or her eyes which are smeared. Either way, even the sky looks hungover.

She sips from the glass of stale, oxidising water on the nightstand and lays down again, pulls the covers up around her head, flips the pillow and buries her face in the cold side, wishing she could remember the last time she'd put a cork back in a bottle. Her greasy, marinated skin suggests it was too long ago to remember.

Cassie could have sworn she didn't doze, but she was woken an hour later by an increasingly muggy day and an abused system that needed a formal apology, preferably by way of extensive rehydration. The more she thought about it the more she could feel cool, fresh water run down the back of her throat, how refreshing and clean it would taste, and she knew that even if she could wait for the drink, she now couldn't wait to pee.

She stretched and recoiled instantly as her foot touched something cold and hard right at the end of the bed. What the hell was that? But then she saw the empty ice-cream tub on the table and realised there was a good chance she had passed out again, still clutching a spoonful of melting sludge, only too susceptible to the forces of gravity and drink. She fumbled for the cutlery, peeling it away from the sheet.

In another life he would have taken it before she dropped it. Not only that, but he'd have taken a photo of her smeary face and left it, adorned with kisses, on the fridge for her to blush at when she finally started what he laughingly called her working day. But he wasn't here to take it, was he?

No thought of him came easily. Maybe they never would. Cassie blinked back tears, very awake now. The first conscious thought of him, every day, meant sleep was at least a bottle of wine away. Wearily she sat up, only to be sorry she had when she saw the miserable woman in the mirror stare balefully at her across the pigsty of a bedroom.

That woman needed a few severe words, but Cassie was pretty sure she wasn't up to the job. She wiped the tears and snot away, stepping onto a floor littered with laundry and corks and dirty dishes, and reluctantly made her way into the bathroom, there to berate her broken heart with what passed for a pep talk these days.

She got as far as the hall, where she slumped against the wall and slid to the floor, hugging her knees to her body and keening his name, over and over.

**Sssh, Cassie. I know it hurts, but it'll be worth it.**

She didn't know how long she had lain like that, but she had to do something about her hangover. Alka Seltzer in one hand, pint of chilled water in the other, she finally faced the wretch in the bathroom mirror, pulled some faces, tried to smile, gave up and went back to bed.

After the rarity of four hours uninterrupted, dreamless sleep she woke again. She felt better. It was too soon for good, she knew, but better was something she could live with.

She got up and checked the clock on her cell, realising there was nearly eight hours to go until she had to face the evening. The ritual that awaited her filled her with dread and the end result seemed abhorrent, but, she acknowledged grudgingly, resentful of hearing Jen and her counsellor say it so often, it was a plan. She sloped back to the bathroom and began to run a bath.

The mirror fogged over as the tub filled and she watched her image fade until all she could see was her own ghost. It seemed appropriate – here but not really here. Reading the back of the bottle of green stuff Jen had brought two days before, Cassie was pretty sure the manufacturers of the bubble bath designed to 'soothe and rejuvenate' had never had terminal grief in mind, but anything was worth a shot and she tipped half the contents under the running taps. Then she bent down, stuck an elbow in the water and decided to risk it.

Shrugging out of her baggy pyjamas she stepped into the bath. She stood for a moment then dropped down to her haunches and gradually stretched her legs out and let the heat send shivers through her as she sank into the soothing warmth.

As she lay back, she listened for the cork popping, but remembered, always a moment too late, that no-one would be bringing her wine. Would her mind ever adjust to this? Eighteen months, give or take, yet the pain seemed no less. She stared down the length of what bits of her pale body were visible through the bubbles and wondered why on earth she had agreed to this nightmare tonight. Getting dressed was hard enough, but smiling? Small talk? She felt the scowl become slightly more entrenched at the appalling thought of it all. Maybe she should just call and cancel… The thought sparked and shimmered, hanging in the air before her. As ever, the temptation to stay on this side of a locked door was like a physical presence in what passed for her life these days. No-one would blame her, she knew. With the smallest sigh, she reached over the edge of the bath and fumbled about on the mat for her cell but jumped as the damn thing rang. She knew who it was without looking at the display and with a rueful sigh she pressed the green button. Resistance was futile.

The voice on the phone was soft and careful.

'You in the bath?'

'Mmf.'

'Well, I guess five hours early is better than an hour late…'

'Jen...'

She was cut off mid-breath, but gently. 'We had this conversation. You said that under no circumstances was I allowed to let you wriggle out of this, remember? You promised me.'

The vehemence of Cassie's response sounded harsh even to Jen. 'Was there an empty bottle on the floor when I said this, Jen? Because I may have been feeling brave, stupid, drunk and defenceless. That ever fucking occur to you? You think this is easy for me? At least you can still whine at yours whenever the bloody mood takes you.'

Jen let that one ride.

Cassie couldn't believe she'd said it out loud, let alone meant it.

'Ah, god, Jen I'm sorry...I didn't sleep much last night and just the thought of dressing up...' Her voice cracked and she sat up, hugging her knees and trying not to cry.

'I know, hon, and I'm gonna be there to hold your hand. And we don't have to stay late. Come out, hate it, drink too fast and be rude to some people. You know you want to.' (At this at least, Jen thought, there was something that might have been a laugh.) 'And when it's all over I'll pour you in the back of a cab, push you up the stairs, shove you into the bathroom and hold your hair while you're sick. I won't even eat your secret chocolate stash in the linen cupboard.'

'The linen cupboard only has sheets in it. That's the week it's been. Anyway, do I have any choice?'

'Of course you do. If you really can't face it, call me at the last minute and bail. Take all the damn time you need. We'll all still be here when you're good and ready. But this was your idea, remember? Now go do what you gotta do and call me later. Love you.'

And the phone was dead. Cassie dropped it unceremoniously back on the mat and closing her eyes, lay back and slid down till just her chin rested on the bubbles.

An hour later, she felt oddly revived. Not exactly excited, but prepared, just maybe, to challenge herself a little. Snuggled in a huge bathrobe with an equally huge glass of wine in one hand, she wandered several times through all the rooms of the flat, circling until she finally sat down in front of the PC.

The first thing she did was email her boss.

'I'm bored, so I'm just emailing you to distract you from whatever you're doing. I'm drinking wine. Did I mention I was bored? Give me something to do. I won't do it, but it'd be good to have something to avoid. Email, don't call…'

She sat back and rested her feet on the desk. She'd barely taken a sip of wine when there was a ping, and a message.

'Folder of images attached. Pick the best one. You need anything, just call. The answer's always no. By the way, I gave your job to an eighteen-year-old with big tits and no talent...'

Despite herself, she grinned at the email. Only Gordon would dare pull this crap.

She replied.

'I miss you too, you old hack.'

The reply took less than a minute. 'Feel free to kick the eye-candy's bony ass out your chair as soon as you feel up to it. All the old hacks miss you.'

Cassie speed-dialled two.

'Hey Jen,' she said as the background sounds of chaos filtered down the line.

A hand over the receiver, 'I have to take this.'

'Bad time?'

'Never a bad time for you. How you doing?'

'OK, for the moment. I haven't burned the dress or anything. I just wanted to say sorry, you know, for the dig earlier. I didn't mean it. You and Mac have been my sanity and it means the world to me. I would've...I mean I could've...I mean...ah Christ, I'm just grateful I have you both, you know?'

A pause, and Cassie heard a door being closed.

'We know. Sweetheart, everyone wants to help, but they're afraid to intrude. It's your call, and always has been. Which reminds me — Mac's visiting baby brother, the cute one, wants to know if you want him to be your stunt date tonight.'

'Tell him that's sweet, and no thanks. I'm sure there's a twenty-two-year-old somewhere needs his services more than me. Besides, it wouldn't feel right, I mean…'

'No explanation necessary. I already told him no, anyway.'

She smiled. 'Jen, I owe you.'

'You owe me nothing. Now fuck off, I'm supposed to look busy today. Remember, everything's OK. Think good thoughts. I'll pick you up at seven.'

**Today is a big day for us.**

Cassie hung up, thinking back to her first nights alone in the apartment, when Jen had refused to leave. To begin with there had been nothing but crises, although none of it seemed to have been too much for Jen. All Cassie could remember of much of the first year was Jen being her physical and emotional prop through every hellish waking moment, when Cassie couldn't believe a heart could break so hard a second time. When standing was beyond her, Jen held her up. When she couldn't speak, Jen made sounds she understood. When Cassie threw up for a week, Jen washed, held and comforted her. When Cassie felt herself slide away from this world and its pain, Jen had held her and spoken softly to whatever survival instinct still lurked within Cassie's broken shell.

And then the first anniversary, a time that Cassie remembers with sometimes alarming clarity although she does her damndest to forget. When she had resurfaced, disappointed that she still seemed to be breathing despite her strongest desire not to be, there was Jen. Never angry or impatient, just always there, absorbing all that was too much for Cassie to contain. It continuously amazed Cassie that all this support came from the shy girl she'd befriended across a garden fence twenty years before. A girl who, eyes averted, would only whisper a timid invitation to play was now the emotional prop Cassie is sure she would have died without. A girl that she had treated so shamefully, time and again, who still thought there was something in Cassie worth sticking around for.

Cassie decided, as she wiped more tears away, that the night was on, regardless. She did owe Jen. No matter how much she didn't want to do this, her best friend deserved a little recognition.

She grabbed the phone again, called the posh sandwich shop underneath Jen's office and ordered her favourite PMS-justifiable steak sandwich with mustard, gravy, onions and extra cheese (with a diet coke), and had them sent up to her.

Drained, she went back to bed.

As she made a feeble effort to smooth out the sheet and duvet, Cassie saw the case in the corner of the room and slumped down onto the edge of the bed. Her scarlet silk throw was still in there, and would stay there for the time being. He should be here to drape it around her and kiss the back of her neck – the last thing they ever did before leaving the house for a night on the tiles. Dancing home in pre-dawn light, he would snatch it away, then loop it around her neck when she turned to face him, and draw her close. She would feign resistance, but wrapped in his arms, their kisses would make her feel as if they were the only two people on earth. She knew in her heart she could never bear to wear it again.

I hear the bed creaking but no tears this time. Maybe you are too exhausted. In all this time, I have only moved from here to shop, choosing instead to be with you, as much as I can be, while you grieve. I couldn't bear for you to go through that without me, all alone. But it will be worth it, I promise you. Every day you are getting closer and closer to where you need to be; to where I need you to be. And now we're so close. You need to make the effort tonight but you have the same weakness of all women and I know it'll be too much for you. Once you fail tonight, I will make it all better.

Cassie set her alarm for six, pulled the covers around her and fell almost instantly into a fragile sleep.

Her dreams were nonsense. She was in an elevator, a forest, then a car, then a pool then a movie theater, but all the while she was looking for Paul because she could hear him shout her name. Then the dream changed and it was something else entirely that called out to her, reached for her, clawed its way to its feet and stumbled around a darkened room, tripping blindly, grabbing for her, and every impulse was to be as far away from this creature as she could run.

When she awoke, she'd been crying and the sheets were clammy. Looking at the empty side of the bed, the only noises choking from her were bits of his name, over and over. She felt a familiar panic surge through her, making her shake and spasm, and on reflex her slippy hands grasped the phone, and fumbling, she speed-dialled two.

'…JEN?…' and then nothing, because the words wouldn't come.

'I know,' said the voice on the other end, 'I know. Ssshhh. Cassie, it's OK,' over and over, Jen repeated her name, soothed, quieted and calmed. 'I'll be over in twenty minutes. Go wash your face, sweetheart. Don't hang up.'

**Always Jen. You'll never be able to do anything alone, ever again. Soon it'll be me you beg to look after you.**

Cassie kept the phone with her, vaguely hearing

Jen saying all the right things as she stumbled from the bedroom and past the kitchen door. The summer evening light bathing the room caught her off-guard and she finally drew a full breath, irrationally relieved there was still daylight. She propped herself against the door-frame, lifting the receiver.

'See you when you get here,' she managed, then hung up, crumpled onto the kitchen floor and wept.

In less than fifteen minutes, I heard footsteps hurry past my door, then a key in your lock.

# Chapter Twenty-Eight

Jen came through the door and flung several bags on the floor. She walked straight into the kitchen, dropped to her knees and held the sobbing Cassie close.

**That noise is what reassures me that it's all gonna work out the way I want. You are doing so well.**

When they pulled apart, Jen brushed a few hairs from her friend's tear-streaked face. 'It's just as well that snot is the new black, otherwise I couldn't take you anywhere.'

Cassie did something which might have been a smile.

'Go shower,' said Jen, 'and I'll go replenish the stash. Don't make me come in there and check behind your ears,' and with that she headed for the linen closet.

Ten minutes later, Jen gently knocked on the unlocked bathroom door and then went right on in without waiting. She sat on the laundry basket until the water was turned off, then when the shower curtain twitched she held up a huge bath towel for Cassie to step into. She stood with her arms around her for a little time, holding Cassie's head to her shoulder, gently running her fingers through her wet hair. After a little while, Cassie sat on the laundry basket while Jen gently brushed her long hair, tying it back into a loose ponytail. Neither woman spoke. Cassie was subdued but no longer tearful and Jen knew to keep quiet and wait. She carried on brushing, listening to Cassie's breathing settle, then she led her back to the sanctuary of her bedroom.

An hour later, both women stood before the bedroom mirror while one admired both their reflections.

Jen had her arm around her friend's waist and, looking only in the mirror, said, 'I have something for you,' and with that she reached behind her and opened one of her bags, handing over a large, soft gift-wrapped package.

'Don't be offended, we just wanted to make it easier.'

Cassie gently prised it open and pulled out a velvet wrap, in a slightly deeper red than the dress.

'Wear the other to make you smile when you think about him, but not tonight. Tonight is therapy, not pleasure. It's not meant to replace his, it's just…an alternative.'

Cassie smiled and turning to Jen she said, 'It's perfect, and how could I be offended? This is the sweetest thought.'

'Actually, if I'm being honest, it was Mac's idea,' and with that, Jen took the wrap and draped it around Cassie's shoulders, and stood holding her, watching her face in the mirror and feeling a gentle shudder run through her. Emotionally drained and feeling redundant, she knew she would give anything to actually, physically, take Cassie's pain and give her back her heart. She bent her head to Cassie's shoulder and breathed slowly, willing the tears back where they came from.

After a moment, Jen stepped back as Cassie reached for the phone, and speed-dialled one.

'Mac?'

'Hey beautiful, what can I do for you?'

'You already do so much. The wrap is beautiful. I love it, and I love that you thought of getting it for me. It was the sweetest thing, and he would have appreciated you caring for me, you know that.' She paused, drawing a deep but wobbly breath. 'And Mac? I know I'm not the only one who misses him.'

'Ach phooey,' said the enormous Swede on the other end of the phone. 'Oh, and tell that wench of mine that if she gets any offers tonight, I won't accept anything less than five camels.' With that he blew her something which sounded like it was meant to be a kiss, and then the line went dead.

'How many camels does he expect to get for me these days?' asked Jen.

'Five. Your stock's gone up, babe.'

Both women stood just inside Cassie's front door with Jen feeling increasingly guilty at the thought that perhaps she had forced this night, that Cassie really wasn't ready, that it would end up doing more harm than good.

Cassie, thinking exactly the same thing, turned to look her friend in the eye. 'It's my choice to do this, Jen. And yeah, I feel sick and guilty and panicked and I would give good money to go back inside and get into bed. I don't feel ready, but I'm never going to feel ready, am I? So...catch me when I fall?'

Jen smiled and kissed her friend on the cheek. 'Always and forever,' and both girls smiled. It had been Cassie's answer when Jen asked her, aged eight, how long they would be friends for.

'Cab for Hollier?' The girls nodded and climbed in.

'Museum Station, right?' he asked, addressing his question directly at Cassie, but it was Jen who answered. 'Yeah, thanks. Just park where you can.'

But as the cabbie sat letting the engine idle, Jen

demanded, 'what are you waiting for?'

'Your friend needs to put her belt on, OK?' he said, twitching his head in Cassie's direction. She'd already wound the window right down and was resting her head on the sill. Her eyes were closed, she was clutching Jen's hand and her breathing was all over the place.

'When I want a lesson from Elmer the Road Safety Elephant, I'll ask for one,' Jen snapped. 'Just fucking drive!'

Cassie raised her head slightly, focused on Jen and said, 'You swore!'

'Oh shush,' grinned Jen, 'and besides, didn't Elmer teach you a damn thing?' Jen made her arm a trunk that she waved from in front of her nose. 'Put your seatbelt on!'

Both girls dissolved in fits of relieved giggles.

As the cab pulled away, Cassie concentrated on her breathing, telling herself over and over that she could do this, she was in control, this was a choice and it was all going to be OK, wishing she could believe just one word of it.

**I was pressed against the door as you went past, picturing you, imagining I could smell your scent. I'll see you so very soon.**

The journey seemed over in a flash but thankfully once there, they disembarked a safe distance from the assembling weekend crowds. Jen paid the by now very sullen cabbie, then gently took her friend's hand and led her towards the main entrance of the Museum, beginning to explain just what would happen when they made it to the party.

'It's a charity bash, so mostly out-of-towners. We have these clients who've just decided to invest in Third World child health programmes, but not before they chuck a huge and tasteless party to ensure that all the other great and good are left in no doubt whatsoever just how Christian and charitable they are.'

'Naturally,' said Cassie.

'It's technically a fundraiser,' continued Jen, 'but bottom line, it's a great cause which I already donated to. But truth be told I've always wanted to come to a party here, so I figure we go help loosen some purse-strings and then leave with a clear conscience and a skin-full.'

'Now tell me the rest,' said Cassie quietly, looping her arm through Jen's.

'We'll be an exhibit, for a while, cos the place is still open to the public. It'll feel weird. I guess it's too damn expensive to hire a whole room, so I think we just have one roped-off area at the back of the Grand Hall, but we will have our own champagne bar, so that's OK. The entire place will be full of eligible, wealthy bachelors all expecting the women to worship them and their donations. You won't know anyone there and I'll know only a few. I was planning on being mostly honest and introducing you as a free-lance photographer. Don't be mad, but I stole some of your cards from the apartment and brought them with me. No-one says you have to take any commissions, but it can't hurt to make gullible rich people aware of you, can it?'

Cassie stopped, so Jen had no choice. For the longest minute she wasn't sure if Cassie was going to break down in tears or punch her, but, after a minute, Cassie just nodded and started walking again.

When they got to the front steps, Cassie said, 'My cards?' and Jen reached into her bag and handed them over. Cassie held them in the palm of her hand, just staring at them as if she'd never seen them before.

She looked up at Jen, laughing gently. 'You should see the look on your face, angel,' she chided. 'I don't know if I can, but you can tell that shrink of mine it was a good try.'

And with that, they climbed the steps, allowed the liveried doorman to escort them to the Grand Hall, where they made their way directly to the champagne bar, and took the edge off. Repeatedly.

It took longer than I thought to shave off all the facial hair. I had to be super-careful because turning up with

**little cuts all over my face was a little more conspicuous than I intended to be. When I was done, I barely recognised myself. The suit had been a donation to the shelter. It had taken me days of door-stepping in the wealthy neighbourhoods till I'd gotten something that fit well.**

Jen leant in to Cassie. 'You be OK for a minute?'

'What? Oh, huh…yeah, sure,' said Cassie, only processing what Jen had said after she found herself alone with two strange men. One sipped his drink and the other smiled at her. The sound of his inhalation as he prepared to speak sounded to Cassie like the fetid pant of some slavering predator standing over a fresh kill.

'So you're a photographer, eh?' he said, winking. Cassie could feel a laugh bubble up out of her, certain it would sound as hysterical as it felt. She nodded and swirled her glass, listening to the gentle fizzing in the silence.

'Portraits?'

'Abandoned industrial landscapes for pleasure,' said Cassie, 'corporate whores for cash. My card,' she added, holding one out to him. He took it, missing the insult, but Cassie watched emptily as his friend grinned and drank deep to suppress the laugh. She knew in another life she'd already be half-way to a cab with him, but not now. He made eye contact with her and smiled properly. She nodded.

'I'm just a corpse-in-waiting,' she thought, 'you're wasting your time.'

# Chapter Twenty-Nine

**You are wearing the red dress. I knew you would. You are wearing it for me.**

To be honest, I would have preferred it if you had failed at home; if maybe you hadn't been able to even get dressed or leave the house. But here you are, and despite the inconvenience, I am eager to see you fail in public. It will be so much more conclusive.

Jen came back and picked up the conversation, allowing Cassie to tune out. She'd drunk herself sober and the two guys they were talking to held no interest for her whatsoever. Jen was happy to do most of the talking and the increasing volume of the room was enough to excuse Cassie any real contribution. She nodded when they did, smiled as much as she could stand and allowed every passing champagne waiter to refresh her glass.

**You think those guys would understand your pain? They have no idea what you have been through. I care, Cassie. I understand you. I know you better than you know yourself.**

Cassie realised, suddenly, that Jen and the men were looking at her.

'I'm sorry,' she smiled, 'I was miles away. What did I miss?'

Jen touched her elbow and made strong eye contact, which she held while one of the men repeated his joke. They all laughed again, this time Cassie joined in.

She was surprised, then horrified, at how easily the laugh came. Everything about it felt alien – even her face felt like it was making strange shapes and she tried to remember if this was always how she laughed. It was hard to know.

**You were doing so damn well, but…oh Cassie, don't fuck this up. Not now. Not after everything I've been through. How can you laugh?**

She turned to Jen and with a huge smile, pulled her close and kissed her on the cheek. She deposited her glass on a passing empty tray and leaned in to the two men and shook their hands. As goodbyes were being said, one of them cracked another terrible joke and all four laughed.

**You think those guys like you? You think…oh, god Cassie, how can you laugh? What was so fucking funny? You think I've done everything I've done for us just so you could laugh with some dumb bastard?**

**I'll show you what fucking pain really means, Cassie.**

Does that idiot care how much pain you are in? Does he give a damn?

How could you do this to me, to us? After all my work, my preparation, the care and love and fucking effort I put into this. This was for us! More than two years of my life! You think this was easy? You think…you think it was random? You think you're the only one to suffer, to feel any kind of pain? You ungrateful bitch! After all I've done for us!

You think you can just disappoint me? Dismiss me? Abandon me? You weren't supposed to do this, Cassie. This is not my plan. I broke you and I meant to break you for good. None of this means anything if you get better, and I will not let you ruin this much work. It was all so perfectly planned. And this is my reward for all that care and attention?

I chose to break you, Cassie, because I needed someone I knew could never be fixed; someone who would finally understand me. Tonight was supposed to be too much for you. Just this one last test, that's all you had to pass. Just this one little thing for me, for ME!

And now look at you. Just how fucking funny is your life, Cassie? Are you actually flirting? All dressed up and painted like the whore you are.

You're no use to me if you get better.

# Chapter Thirty

As Jen took their wraps from the coat-check and said a few final goodbyes, Cassie left the party by a side door and waited on the dark, deserted grass verge. She turned her back to the door, feeling tears coming and not wanting to be seen.

Within minutes, she felt Jen's arms around her, draping the stole across her shoulders.

'I'm exhausted.'

'We could have left any time, you know that, right?' Jen's voice held real concern – she hadn't intended for them to stay long, but Cassie had seemed OK. Still, for a first time out it seemed a bit much.

'It's OK, though,' said Cassie, 'just…I'm just surprised. At myself, mostly. It was like acting…like if I could fool these people into thinking I was OK, then maybe I would start to believe it, you know?'

Jen nodded. 'You're not OK though, are you?'

Cassie looked away, utterly drained at the sheer effort of it all. 'No, babe,' she said through her tears, 'I'm not OK. I'm dead inside and it's only cowardice and you that stops me making that permanent. My one true love was torn apart by a maniac eighteen months ago. Sometimes I think I hear him call me but when I answer, there's just silence. Sometimes I think I see him from the window and I run out into the street but he's always gone. And what makes it worse is you taking it all and it's never too much and you give me so much but what you don't know, what you'll never really know, is that the woman you love is dead and all that's left is me, rotting in my fucking misery and it's never going to stop because I died when he did, but no-one had the decency to bury me and let me be!'

Cassie paced and ranted, clawing her arms and half-choking on her own words while Jen stood very still, silent tears running down her face until she sat down on the doorstep, hugged her knees to her chest and sobbed.

**Where the hell are you? You wouldn't actually stay, would you…?**

Eventually Jen felt an arm around her shoulders and warm breath on her ear.

'Baby I'm sorry,' Cassie whispered. 'I'm so sorry. Look at me, please. Look at me, there's something I need to say to you.'

Cassie crouched, held Jen's face in her hands, kissed her lightly on one cheek, looked into her eyes and said, 'Thank you. I'd be dead without you, and as awful as life is, I don't want to be dead.'

She stood up, holding Jen's hand, helping her to her feet. They both leant against the building, watching the sky. 'The thing that freaks me out the most is that some nights I lie there wondering if Paul died because I deserved something truly bad to happen to me. What if it was my fault?'

Jen sniffed. 'Are you serious? That's really what you think? Oh, Cassie…'

'Just sometimes,' said Cassie quietly. 'Like I lie there thinking about the million things I should have done better, and I wonder if this is my wake-up call.'

'It wasn't your fault. The only person that can be held responsible is the person that did it. You loved Paul and he loved you.' She brushed a stray hair from Cassie's face. 'You did a big thing coming out tonight and it was always going to make you feel bad, and I am so proud of you for doing it. You are not always going to feel this bad, I promise.'

Arm in arm they very slowly walked along the thin path that ran the length of the main hall, finally coming out halfway down the front steps.

**There you are. Whore.**

The girls walked home in silence through the still summer night. Soon it was only a couple of blocks to Cassie's apartment and they stood waiting to cross the junction, watching lots of available cabs drive past.

'I need to walk, and I'd like to go home alone.'

Jen wasn't happy with that and said as much, but Cassie seemed different after her outburst and quite determined that she could end the night unaided.

Jen still took some convincing but Cassie was in no mood to argue and promised to call her the next day. Jen stepped up to her, wrapped her arms around her and held her close, then turned and hailed a cab. As it pulled away, she turned to watch Cassie as she disappeared out of sight. Right then all she wanted was to see Mac, to hold him, to make sure he was really there, to let him know that it could so easily have been her in Cassie's place, and tell him just how much she loved and needed him.

Fifteen minutes later Cassie stepped gratefully into the darkness of her hall and leant against the closing door as it clicked shut. Every inch of her felt heavy. She didn't know what to think about tonight. She knew that on a good day, soon, she would have to admit to herself and maybe others that it hadn't been as bad as she had anticipated. And she knew that as soon as she admitted it, she would be expected to do it again. And again and again and again. All she really wanted to do was curl up in bed and apologise to Paul for having ever agreed to go. It felt like a guilty secret, a lie, an infidelity. It was disrespectful and selfish and shallow. She was in mourning and had gone to a fucking party.

'I'm drunk and too tired to beat myself up tonight,' she said to the dark apartment and walked unsteadily to the kitchen where she drank some OJ straight from the bottle by the light of the open fridge, then went to bed, taking the juice with her. The room was softly lit by the never-night of high Summer and she stepped out her shoes, let her beautiful, expensive, delicate dress fall to the floor over them and unceremoniously dropped her underwear on top of the pile.

Sitting on the edge of the bed, watching the moon through the curtains, she drank the OJ and thought about her breathing. She spoke to the empty room.

'Baby I had to go. I didn't want to, but I had to. I felt so bad being there without you, and I missed you so much I couldn't bear it.' She paused, drew breath. 'How the hell am I supposed to do this without you?'

Tears running down her face she put the bottle on the table and tucked her feet up under the duvet, pulling the edges of it around her, hugging herself. She lay watching the stars, sobbing quietly, feeling the evening's alcohol work its soporific magic through her system, and then her drying eyes began to close.

# Chapter Thirty–One

To come so close, only to fail at the very last. Well, you can't blame me for being angry about that, can you?

It hurts.

Oh, Shauna. I waited such a long time for you to come to me.

Of course, I know there was never really any you. There was only me.

I can't believe it took me such a long time to realise what an idiot I was being – I didn't need anything to have actually hapened to me, I just needed other people to believe that something had happened, and let them do the work for me.

For practice, I bought a pawned wedding ring and made regular forays into distant neighbourhoods where I would hang out in the back rows of churches, some-times waiting entire days in the dim cool for just the right person to stop by. When they did, I'd alter my breathing, sniff loudly, sob a little too audibly, all the while running my poor-dead-Shauna fantasy over and over in my mind until I'd worked myself into a seemingly authentic state. Somebody would always come to ask if I was alright.

The first time out, it worked like a dream.

'He knocked her down.' I looked away for a moment. 'On her way back from seeing our midwife.' I heard a gasp. 'He reversed over her. Drove over her again. Back and forth. There was so little of her left.' I snapped my head up and stared into the woman's eyes. 'She looked like roadkill.' Keeping a straight face was difficult enough but at the look of horror and pity on her face I could feel the stirrings of an erection. I pulled my hand from hers. I wanted very badly to laugh out loud. As the moment passed, I thanked her for her kindness, told her I had to leave and walked blinking into the sunshine. There were so many other churches to visit.

Months of this and it became my truth. I moved again and, having easily identified the women I could rely on to spread my news, let the gossip networks inform my new neighbours of my tragic past.

They were so damn nice to me. So sympathetic. I liked how they baked me cakes and invited me to their homes and made sure their kids helped me with my garden, took my trash out and painted my fence. I told them, Shauna, that you were my childhood sweetheart and how we ran away from our parents and got married real young. That made them extra nice to me. From there it was fun.

'She was pregnant. I mean, we were pregnant. We wanted three kids.'

'Oh, I'm so sorry. I can't imagine anything more awful.'

'Thank you. I came so close to losing my faith. It's hard to believe when you see what he did to her.'

I used to count my heartbeats until they asked my favourite question. This was the bit I loved. See, it's like rubber-necking at a traffic accident. All they wanted was the juiciest gossip, the goriest details. Then they could gloat over their friends and neighbours. I never gave them the satisfaction. Instead I would hang my head, willing tears to come, not looking up again until my eyes were moist and my voice was thick.

'Maybe I could have stopped him. Maybe she would still be here if I'd done things differently.'

And every time, the great absolution.

'You mustn't blame yourself.'

I loved that. I even invented anniversaries of both our weddding and her death, just to hear it more often. Oddly, I used to get quite upset on those days.

With so many people encouraging me to move on, to love again, telling me over and over that I deserved to be happy, I knew I was ready to start over. It was time to start looking for a nice girl to take the place of my perfect, dead, pregnant, pretend wife.

Except that it's been frustrating trying to engineer

perfection and just when I had the chance to turn it all around, it's been ruined by you, Cassie. You've hurt me, but worse than that, you've disappointed me.

You did so well for so long. Really, so much better than all the others. But in the end you're just like them, Cassie, because you've failed me, and like Emily and Rachel and Nell before you, you'll pay for that.

I can't have you recover, do you see? Where would that leave me?

# Chapter Thirty-Two

Numbed and drifting, consciousness was the far shore when Cassie heard a key in the lock.

She heard a noise, like something heavy being dragged over wood, but she was too sleepy to know whether it was a leftover sound from her dream.

Sitting up in bed she listened hard, willing her eyes to adjust to the gloom. There was something weird about the silence.

She heard the soft click of her front door closing again.

'Jen?'

Not getting a reply, Cassie reached across the nightstand and clicked the lamp on, turning to look at the bedroom door, which is when she saw the orchid lying on Paul's pillow.

# Chapter Thirty-Three

Jen stopped at the entrance to her building and sat down on the top step. As much as she wanted to see and hold Mac, she needed a minute. She didn't get it.

The door opened behind her and the ancient decking creaked as Mac stepped out and sat beside her.

'You OK?'

Jen knew if she turned to face him, her composure would collapse for the second time that night. She stared straight ahead, nodding gently.

'Cassie OK?'

Jen drew a breath and sighed, resting her head against Mac's shoulder His arm was around her instantly and she cried quietly while he rocked her gently, his lips in her hair, his kisses warm on her scalp.

After a few minutes she sniffed hard and wiped the tears from her face. She sat up straight and faced Mac, returning his smile.

'I don't know if she is. Tonight was so weird. She wouldn't let me walk her home, but…'

Mac waited. He'd spent so many nights shoring

up what was left of Jen's strength after time spent supporting Cassie that he knew she'd tell him when she was ready.

'I'm just scared for her that it was some huge step backwards, you know? She was starting to take pictures again, even though it was just around the apartment. What if I made her do this and she wasn't ready?'

'You really think even you can make Cassie do anything she doesn't really want to do?'

They both laughed, a little.

'I guess, but you should have seen her when I said goodbye – I've never seen her like that.'

'You want to take a walk over there?'

'D'you mind?'

Mac didn't. He went upstairs and locked their apartment properly, then rejoined Jen on the street, took her hand and led her back the way she'd come.

When she hadn't gotten an answer, Cassie had reached out for the orchid, convinced that she was hallucinating. She couldn't figure out what the hell it was doing there. Paul was dead. Jen would never have done anything so tactless. It couldn't be some ridiculous bit of therapy.

As she held the delicate white and lilac flower in her trembling palm, she heard a noise from the kitchen.

Cassie scrambled out of bed, dropping the orchid amongst the sheets. She skidded on the silk of the crumpled dress, grabbed her jeans and a t-shirt off the back of her chair and fumbled them on.

Breathing hard, she reached into her bedside drawer for the knife that had been there ever since Paul's murder. Trying to grip it in one shaking hand, she took a step towards the bedroom door but froze when it opened towards her.

**Cassie.**

The man stood a little over six feet tall and seemed in no hurry to do anything. His arms hung by his sides and he was smiling.

'Cassie.'

Skirving slid the Taser's trigger safety cover back and took another step into the room.

'I'm over-reacting.'

'Probably.'

'Am I like this with everything?'

'No, just Cassie.'

Jen nodded silent agreement. She looked across the street. 'Shall we go through the park? It's such a gorgeous night. Five more minutes won't kill her.'

'I know you.'

Skirving giggled and shook his head. 'Go on,

then. What's my name?' He took another step towards Cassie and she backed round the bed, into the corner, still clutching the knife.

'Didn't think so. I wanted you to be the one that got it right, Cassie, but you fucked it up.'

Cassie opened her mouth to say something but before she could, Skirving fired.

Instinctively she tried to duck and turn from the probes flying across the room towards her, but the tiny needlepoints made contact with her shoulder and neck. As the electrical signal charged through her for a full five seconds, she lost all muscle control and sank to the floor.

Cassie could feel small, involuntary muscle con-tractions pulse through her hands and feet; aside from a strong tingling sensation in her limbs, she was sure she could move but after her first attempt, she had to hang her head foward to try and clear the over-whelming sense of vertigo. When she opened her eyes, Skirving was standing over her.

He lifted her easily onto the bed, laying her on her side. He moved around out of her line of sight and then she felt something heavy being placed on the bed beyond her head.

Skirving muttered to himself as he rolled out his toolkit, displaying a nightmarish selection of implements and devices that glistened in the lamplight of the room.

Cassie tried to speak, but only the smallest noises would come. All her body would let her do was cry.

Skirving pressed the Taser into Cassie's flesh and shot her a second time.

'It's your own fault, Cassie. You've only yourself to blame.'

Skirving had been too preoccupied to hear a second key in the lock.

'Cassie?' Jen shut the door behind her.

Skirving stopped with a small scalpel in his hand. He had no time. Grabbing the Taser from the floor, he pressed it into Cassie's flesh, shocking her a third time. She shook violently, her body pulled in unnatural directions by the muscle spasms. As the bedroom door opened, Skirving stepped in front of Jen and before she had time to draw breath, he punched her hard on the side of her face. She went down instantly, falling against Mac who stumbled as he tried to catch her. Skirving saw his chance, pressed the stun gun into Mac's side and fired. He clambered past as the man collapsed, then stumbled out into the hallway. He was gone before any of them were able to move.

The wounds on Cassie's arms and shoulders left a trail of blood over the sheets as she kicked the tool kit aside and crawled across the bed, sliding onto the floor where Jen and Mac were regaining consciousness. While the Taser's effects wore off, the relief that all three of them were still alive was enough to get her back across the room to the window. The street was clear. Wincing, she grabbed the phone and dialled 911.

From behind a tree in the park across the street, Skirving watched Cassie's pale face appear briefly at her window. He tried hard to remember what it felt like when she was special but it was as if he was numb. She wasn't the one. But there would always be others.